ROMANCE AT KINGFISHER COVE

ANNE LUCY-SHANLEY

ROMANCE AT KINGFISHER COVE
Copyright © 2024 NINTH AND ARIES PUBLISHING
EBOOK ISBN: 978-1-7366907-6-5
PRINT ISBN: 978-1-7366907-7-2
Editing by EnCompass

To my author friends, with love and gratitude—Amber, Laura, Amanda, Nikol, Jenny, and Patricia

CHAPTER ONE

"Posture, Katrina," Grandmother admonished, dabbing her lips with a linen napkin.

My face prickling, I straightened. After Grandmother's nod of approval, I forked a chunk of lobster into my mouth.

The maid came through the swinging door connecting the kitchen to the dining room, a fresh bottle of chilled chardonnay in hand. She topped off Grandmother's wineglass then rounded the table to Granddad's spot to refill his.

"Can't I have wine, Grandmother? To try?" I begged, adding, "I'm eighteen now."

It was a balmy June day. The ceiling fan above spun lazily. Dean Martin's velvet baritone crooned over the ancient record player on the sideboard. Golden late afternoon sun streamed through the window, kissing Grandmother's rouged cheeks. She picked at her plate of cold seafood salad—light fare was an absolute must when summering on the island—and

1

arched an eyebrow. "Barely, considering your birthday was only last week."

"Oh come now, Frances," Granddad coaxed, winking at me. "Kitty Kat's old enough for a sample of vino."

Grandmother sighed. "Very well. I lack the strength at present to battle you both." She waved a hand at the maid lingering at Granddad's chair. "A *scarce* pour, Sarah."

After leaving a splash of liquid in my goblet, Sarah placed the bottle on the sideboard and fussed with the platter of fruit and cheese that would be served for dessert. I sipped my wine, feeling the epitome of sophistication. I let the flavors saturate my taste buds before swallowing. Unfamiliar but agreeable. Heady. Heat bloomed on my skin.

After everyone retired to bed, I'd sneak into the kitchen to filch a glass. I'd take it down to the beach and listen to the sea. Stargaze. Reflect. I had plenty to contemplate with starting Stayton University in the autumn.

"Sarah, would you mind mixing me a G and T with extra lime?" Granddad downed his chardonnay. "I could use an after-supper cocktail."

"Certainly, Mr. Dumont." Sarah exited the room, heading toward the parlor where the drinks cart was kept.

Grandmother threw Granddad a pointed look. "Dinner. The evening repast is *dinner*, Charles."

"Bah." He turned to me with a twinkle in his eye, grinning mischievously. "I'm a low-class fella. I can't put on airs—it'll always be supper to me."

"And I believe you've had quite enough spirits already. You need a clear head," she continued, "when Geoffrey phones later to review our financials."

I smiled at Granddad, thankful for the thousandth time he wasn't hoity-toity. He'd rejected Grandmother's decree we dress for dinner, his attire a simple, faded polo, and a pair of creased khakis. He didn't care whether he used the wrong fork at meals or rested his elbows on the table. Forty-odd years of marriage to a Randcliffe couldn't shake Granddad's indifference. Refusing to bow to conventions was a testament to Charlie Dumont's humble roots.

A curious tension was building in the room. Watching my grandparents' non-verbal interplay, I twirled the delicate stem of my empty wineglass, my stomach flip-flopping. Granddad was his usual carefree self, but something simmered between him and Grandmother I didn't understand. Something terse. Disturbing.

Was she angry he'd spent another afternoon at the dog track on the mainland?

Sarah returned, ice tinkling in the tumbler she placed beside Granddad's plate. "Your gin and tonic, sir."

Granddad rubbed his hands together in anticipation, then he picked up the drink and took a healthy swig.

"For pity's sake, Katrina! Will you *stop slouching*," Grandmother snapped, and I sat to attention, threading my fingers in my lap.

Sarah collected the dirty dishes and retreated to the kitchen, the skirt of her starched uniform swishing. Evidently, I wasn't the only one feeling the friction hovering like ether.

"Franny," Granddad chided.

The song on the record player finished, the needle bouncing in the stillness of the dining room.

"I detest nicknames." Grandmother's upper lip stiffened. She glared at Granddad. "The least we can provide the child is impeccable manners. The very least, wouldn't you concur?"

She was often taciturn, even severe. Nevertheless, her resentful expression baffled me. Granddad flushed. He looked nervous. Guilty. Their bickering was commonplace but never with this kind of bite. My gaze swiveled between them, my palms dampening.

What was going on?

Granddad patted my arm. "How would you like to take

the wagon into town and buy yourself a sundae, Kitty Kat? Or go for a swim at the club?"

My mouth dropped, surprise displacing my unease. I'd received my license at sixteen but rarely drove, especially alone. Escape Randcliffe Cottage to explore the Cove on my own, this near to dusk? The notion was more intoxicating than the wine I'd consumed. "Really? Can I?"

He shifted forward and pulled his wallet from his back pocket. Thumbing through the bills inside, he took out a twenty, passing it to me. "Don't stay out too late though, my dear."

I chanced a glance at Grandmother. She appeared displeased yet said nothing.

Pushing my chair back with eagerness, I hurried to my bedroom—the room that had been my mother's. Sarah had left folded stacks of clean laundry on the canopy bed. I found my swimsuit, a pair of shorts, and a peasant blouse. Dressing quickly, I gathered my hair into a ponytail.

On my way to the kitchen, I detoured to the parlor to say goodbye to my grandparents. They now sat on the sofa, heads bent close. They didn't notice me—their conversation seemed intense, and their voices were hushed. Something was up, but I wasn't about to let the opportunity for independence slip through my fingers.

Ignoring the weird gnawing in the pit of my belly, I tiptoed away.

CHAPTER TWO

THE ANTIQUATED STATION WAGON'S BRAKES WERE SPONGY FROM disuse. I drove with care away from the cottage along Sand Dollar Way past the gracious, low country-style dwellings with their pastel-hued siding and wraparound verandas. A seagull kept pace with me, sailing alongside the car, the tips of its wing brushing my window. With a short squawk, the gull changed course and flew away.

I turned onto Starfish Avenue, and the residential district morphed into upscale storefronts and eateries. The gelateria adjacent to the fishmonger we frequented was mobbed with sightseers in resort wear, a line forming which stretched to the public access beach. Gelato didn't interest me, and the country club was on the ritzier side of the island, the eastern side.

Silber Sound was on my left, peppered with vacation homes and budget-conscious summer rentals overlooking the water, the mainland beyond. I cranked my window down all the way, the wind tousling my ponytail. Scents rolled in—the tang of fish and the sweet, briny earthiness of kelp abundant in the shallows.

The entrance of the four-lane suspension bridge spanning

the Sound loomed ahead. The isle's tangible connection to the mainland, its construction in 1950 transformed Kingfisher Cove from an exclusive haven for the filthy rich to a vacation mecca within the grasp of the average family.

A dented minivan zoomed from behind me, cutting me off then slowing. I stomped on the brake, and the wagon shuddered. The minivan careened onto the parkway bridge. Frowning, I mimicked what Granddad grumbled in such situations, "Tourists!"

Regardless of the disdain they received, tourists had become the lifeblood of the Cove well before my great-great-great-grandfather built our cottage in the early nineteen-hundreds. The summer home and the Cove were part of me. Part of my DNA. I was *not* a tourist. I'd been staying here every June since infancy and knew the history—an English mariner happened upon the uncharted land mass in the late 1650s while on a surveying expedition. He claimed the island for the crown, naming it after the profusion of small charcoal-gray-and-white birds with untidy crests and dagger-like beaks—the Belted Kingfisher.

There had been few human inhabitants on the island until an industrialist chose to build a retreat here more than two hundred years later. In its heyday, the highest echelon of society flooded his sprawling estate, Shoreside, for functions. In time, it fell into disrepair, and a development company purchased the estate. Now, Shoreside was a fancy private resort. Framed photographs of parties through the years decorated the walls of the reception area—photos prominently featuring *my* forebears.

The stoplight past the base of the bridge went from amber to red. I idled, waiting for traffic. Starfish Avenue wound around the entire island. If I stayed on it, I'd find myself back by our cottage. My intent? To check out Upper Kingfisher, the working-class section where the servants of the wealthy visitors settled at the turn of the twentieth century.

Passing a supermarket vastly dissimilar to our trendy Lower Kingfisher grocer, I glanced around, fascinated. A shrill shriek of a tool drifted from a gas station garage. There were no tasteful souvenir shops or overpriced confectioners. No throngs of vacationers in pricey clothes toting designer lattes while window shopping. Instead, the people here wore jean cutoffs and sneakers, striding purposefully as they went about their business.

Adjoining the marina, a grizzled fisherman with a rust-colored beard filleted his catch of the day on a makeshift plywood countertop. A plump girl in a tube top sold the fisherman's wares by the seawall, looking bored. I recognized the name on the peeling sign above her as that of our fishmonger, O'Flaherty's. These digs were distinctly less extravagant than the shop we bought from.

The majority of the crafts docked at the wharf were working boats. A weathered crabber chugged into the harbor, its pots teeming with blue-tinted crustaceans, a flock of greedy seagulls in its wake. Rather than Coppertone and sugar perfuming the tourist area, the air here was imbued with gasoline and fish guts. Mere miles from home, but another world.

My gaze skated over cafés, restaurants, and a dive bar called The Shanty. Then there were rows of single-family homes shoved together with the narrowest of strips of grass linking them. I cruised through the modest neighborhoods, up a street then down another. In a yard, kids played tag while their father grilled burgers. I wasn't hungry, but my stomach growled at the wafting scent of charred meat.

The sun was beginning to slide down the horizon. The tides would soon recede. My mood turned gloomy. On a whim, I decided to drive to Hollby Lighthouse and take in the sunset.

One lone vehicle remained in the parking lot when I pulled in—lighthouse tours had concluded hours ago. I locked the wagon, my sandals clacking on the blacktop as I walked. The red-and-white edifice was at the northernmost tip of the island, a cement walkway cleaving a path in the patches of seagrass and scrub leading to it. Thick rope woven through posts bordered the path.

I bypassed the lighthouse and the attached addition housing the gift shop, veering left. A wooden bench afforded an obstructed view a short distance from the roped-off cliffs' edges. Breeze lifting my hair, I stood at the precipice, chewing my lip. Here, the cliffs weren't so much cliffs as outcrops of dark stone. If a person was super cautious, they could use the boulders as a stairway. Sitting nearer the lapping water seemed divine.

With a glimpse over my shoulder to ensure I wasn't seen, I gingerly stepped over the rope onto a boulder. Determining it safe, I lowered to another.

Halfway down to my destination, I lost my footing.

CHAPTER THREE

I LET OUT A CRY OF ALARM, MY ARMS FLAILING AS I FELL.

Skidding down the embankment, I splayed my hands. Grabbed at the plumes of oat grass sprouting from between the rocks. My right foot found a sturdy stone. I braced my sandal against it then curled my fingers around the boulder beneath me.

My left leg dangled over space, and my sandal slithered off. I froze, closing my eyes. One wrong move, and I'd plummet into the drink after it.

This is what you get when you step out of your comfort zone and break the rules. Now what are you going to do, genius?

"Hold on!" a deep, honey-toned voice advised from above.

Eyes squeezed shut, I concentrated on staying in place. My temples throbbed from holding my breath, but I didn't dare shift an inch.

The man descended the embankment, promising in a calm tone, "Almost there."

Hands hooked under my armpits and towed me into a solid chest. I rotated, clutching at the man. My limbs trembled, but he held me tight. His shirt was smooth beneath my cheek, the thud of his heartbeat comforting. I exhaled and drew a shaky breath. "Th-thank you."

"What on earth were you thinking bypassing the stanchion and climbing down the embankment? Didn't you see the signs posted?"

I raised my head, opening my eyes. The sun washed him in a tawny aura, causing me to squint. Our gazes met. His irises were moss-green flecked with hazel. Around my age, he was gorgeous—muscular. Bronze-skinned.

Awareness tinkled over me, and I averted my gaze. Pulling away, I shook my head, embarrassment scorching my face. "I-I wanted to sit b-by the water, and I slipped on a rock."

"Lucky I stayed late tonight to do inventory," he said, flicking his shaggy sun-bleached hair from his eyes. His red polo shirt had a lighthouse insignia embroidered in black, along with a name—Jace. "I was leaving when I heard you scream. Can you stand?"

"I-I think so." I inhaled through my nose and blew slowly out my mouth.

Unfolding from the boulder, Jace offered his hand. I grasped it, allowing him to help me to my feet. I put my palms on my kneecaps, dizzy.

"Whoa." He steadied me when I swayed. "Let's get you on land."

We made our way up the embankment. My legs wobbled —I couldn't make them quit wobbling. Jace must've noticed. Mortified, I fought tears. *Why am I such a weakling? God. I'm a loser. A loser!* Swallowing hard, I murmured, "I-I should p-probably go."

"You're in no condition to drive," Jace pointed out. Clearing his throat, he released my arm. He hitched his thumb toward the gift shop. "Wanna rest inside?"

"I-I better not."

"Yeah, you don't know me," Jace said. "You're smart to be

careful."

He was really good-looking. I had limited experience with the opposite sex. Was I woozy from losing footing or because I found him attractive? "The bench is fine."

"After all your trouble, I wouldn't want you to miss the sunset." Jace led me to a rock bed by the lighthouse, flashing a smile that displayed a pearly set of teeth. "This spot'll be perfect. Better than the bench."

Once I was settled, Jace took a keychain from the pocket of his jean shorts. Winking, he said he'd be back in a second. I craned my neck to watch him walk away—the urge to check him out was irresistible—my eyes locking on his butt. *Daaang!* Unbolting the door to the gift shop, Jace disappeared inside. I was still blushing when he returned with two bottles of beer.

"My boss keeps a six-pack in the staff fridge." He twisted the cap off of one and passed it over. "He won't care."

"But I'm not twenty-one."

"Neither am I. Go ahead. It doesn't matter."

I accepted the beer and took a drink, grimacing at the taste.

We sat side by side with our backs to the lighthouse, wordless. It was as if we were in our own bubble, insulated from the world. The breeze was cool and thick with salt, the crashing of the surf against the cliff punctuated by an occasional seagull cawing. Jace drank his beer, the movement of his arm exposing the edges of a tattoo along the cuff of his polo.

I removed my sandal and brought my knees to my chest, my heels sinking into the pebbles underneath us. I held my beer by the neck but did not drink.

By degrees, the orb of the sun vanished, the sky saturated with dramatic smudges of apricot and orange and purple. Jace's shoulder brushed mine when he tipped his bottle to drain his beer, and my skin tingled through the thin fabric of my blouse. We were close enough that I could smell the soapy scent of his cologne. I peeked at him from under my lashes. He had a nice profile—a strong brow, a nose straight as an arrow, and a squared jaw. I marshaled courage. "I'm Katrina."

He turned to me, dusk darkening his eyes. "Jace."

"I know." I nodded to his shirt, and we shared an awkward laugh. "Thanks again for, uh, saving me before."

"Well, it's kinda my job." At my blank look, he elaborated, "Not here. My other job. It's my first summer lifeguarding at Shoreside."

"Oh." *Aren't you the witty conversationalist?*

"Haven't you heard of it? It's pretty famous on the Cove."

"Sure. I've never stayed there, though."

"Most vacationers haven't." Jace put a hand up, rubbing his thumb against the tips of his other fingers to indicate "big money".

"I mean, I've been there. To the tennis courts and stuff. And the pool," I clarified. "I just like the beach more."

"Last two years I was a lifeguard at Cleary Beach, south of the Sound. You know it?" Jace paused until I assented then continued, "Shoreside's got a waitlist for lifeguards. I was about to cave and apply for busboy in one of the restaurants when I got their call. Glad I held out—lifeguards make bank over there."

I recalled Granddad leaving a hundred-dollar tip at brunch the weekend before last at Shoreside's casual dining bistro, The Seafarer. "You should be a waiter at one of the restaurants."

"They only give those jobs to frat boys from the mainland. Lifeguarding or caddying is the only option for guys like me." Jace tossed his head, unconcerned. "Where you stayin'?"

"My family has a house on the island. In Lower Kingfisher."

He whistled. I sensed his manner becoming reserved.

Lower and Upper Kingfisher did not mix.

CHAPTER FOUR

"I'M *NOT* A SNOB." MY WORDS CAME OUT DEFENSIVE. I swallowed and assumed nonchalance. "My parents didn't have a permanent address—they were practically homeless. They didn't have a dime to their names when they died."

"I knew you were cool," Jace assured me, his lip quirking. "It threw me for a minute when you said Lower King."

"I'm definitely cool." I wasn't, but he didn't have to know that, did he? For some reason, Jace viewing me as cool was crucial. "My father was a photographer chasing a Pulitzer, and my mother wanted to be with him more than she wanted to stay with me in the US. They died in Rwanda when I was young. I was raised by my mother's family."

"Sad." Jace studied me. I lifted a shoulder, setting my beer into the pebbles beside me. It *was* sad, but my parents' death wasn't something I brooded over. "You got brothers? Sisters?"

"No. Do you?"

"There are six of us."

"Oh, wow." A rush of yearning swept over me. My childhood was all governesses and ballet classes and piano lessons. Playdates arranged with the grandchildren of my grandparents' friends. I never fit in among my wealthy peers. It had been a lonesome upbringing. "I'm jealous."

He laughed. "Don't be. Our house only had one bathroom when all my brothers were living at home. We fought like dogs and cats over the shower on school mornings until my ma posted a schedule. Pop finally added another bathroom this spring."

"Do you get along with your siblings?"

"Most of the time." Jace readjusted his legs, straightening them. They were long and tanned. He crossed his ankles. "My oldest brother Jackson has a trawler. I go out to help with the nets. Hard work, but it's better than any gym."

That explained his brawny biceps. I listened to Jace's stories about working on Jackson's boat. Then, I talked about how I was enrolled in college and moving into my dorm mid-August. "I'm a legacy student. The women in my family have been going there since it was founded. A library is named after my great-grandmother."

"Damn. Y'all must be loaded." Jace observed dryly, "You don't want to go to that school."

"It's not as if it's my choice, is it? I have to go."

"Do you?"

"Yes." I sighed. My feelings were not often taken into consideration. Attending college was one of a long list of obligations I had to fulfill. The familiar suffocating heaviness on my chest told me to steer clear of discussing emotions, but Jace was an excellent listener. I forced the words out, knowing instinctively he wouldn't judge me. "I get why my mother eloped after graduation. Why she preferred to be a nomad. Being an only child of an only child is a lot of responsibility…"

"Your mom did things her way," Jace said, his voice gentle. "Why can't you?"

I shrugged as if I didn't know why I couldn't, but I did. I

wasn't brave enough to stand up to Grandmother. "What about you? Are you going to school in the autumn?"

"Naw. I'm going into the family biz. I just gotta get licensed. What's your major?"

"My grandmother is pressuring me to pursue medicine or law. Neither field piques my interest."

"You're gonna be alright," Jace said. "You're the most grown-up teenager I've ever met."

I didn't respond. I'd always been too grown-up. Too serious. It made me an outcast sometimes.

Inky twilight settled over us like a shawl, the susurration of the waves hypnotic. I shifted against the lighthouse, the surface of it rough against my back. Picking up a handful of pebbles, I let them trickle through my fingers then grabbed another handful. A sharp prick of pain made me gasp.

I lifted my hand. A drop of blood bloomed on my index finger.

"Lemme see," Jace instructed, taking my hand in his and bringing it to his face to inspect it. "It's not so bad."

"Sharp stone." I realized we were inches away. Time halted, our breath intermingling. Jace put my finger to his mouth and sucked the blood from it.

Our gazes held. I was convinced my heart had ceased beating. Sweet Jesus. It was the most erotic thing I'd ever experienced.

Removing my finger from his mouth, Jace leaned forward and planted his lips on mine.

CHAPTER FIVE

JACE TASTED OF BEER, HIS KISS CONFIDENT BUT RESTRAINED.

His lips probed mine. I was caught off guard, unsure how to respond. My pulse jackhammered, making my ears thunder in cadence with my heartbeat. The heat of his skin radiated onto mine, warming me. Should I try to return his kiss? Should I touch him? All I was certain of was that I liked what Jace was doing.

His hands cradled my face, drawing me even closer. I rested my palms on his shoulders, holding my breath as the tip of his tongue touched mine, excitement blazing fire in my bloodstream.

Romance novels had never enchanted me. I shook my head at my classmates tittering over their schoolgirl crushes. Dates set up with Grandmother's friends' grandsons left me cold. I loathed how during school dances those clowns inevitably fumbled to cop a feel then got belligerent when I told them to knock it off. No, I never fathomed the appeal of guys—they weren't worth the hassle. Not then. Not before this night… before Jace and the magic of being in his arms.

I didn't know his last name, but now everything shifted into focus—it was clear. Now I got it. With Jace, I was unencumbered, free to concentrate solely on what felt good. To forget everything and live in the moment. Each invigorating, exhilarating second.

Pulling away, Jace traced the curve of my cheek with the back of his hand. "How long you stayin' at the Cove?"

"All June," I whispered, breathless.

"That's great news—best I've had all week." His voice was tinged with pleasure, transforming to regret when he added, "It's gettin' late."

I felt my face fall with disappointment. I didn't want this night to end. Everything about the way Jace looked at me told me he felt the same. "I know... I ought to get home."

"Listen, I lifeguard at Shoreside from nine 'til five tomorrow. Can I take you out after work?"

"Like on a... a date?"

"Yeah." Jace grinned. "A date. Think your family will be cool with that?"

No. I didn't think that at all, but I was willing to do anything to go out with Jace. If I couldn't come up with a plausible excuse to leave the house, I'd risk sneaking out. "Sure."

"Meet me at the main gate at 5:15? We'll pick up a pizza at Gino's and take it to the beach at the bird sanctuary."

Jace escorted me to the wagon, waiting while I unlocked the driver's side door. He positioned his hand on the jamb to stop me from slipping inside the car then stepped into me, bending to kiss me again. Intuition my guide, I moved my lips against his. Burying my fingers in his shirt, I clung to him when he deepened the kiss.

When Jace broke away, he placed his forehead lightly against mine. "Do you believe in fate, Katrina?"

Clearing my throat, I murmured, "I-I do now."

Jace smiled, sidestepping to hold the door for me. "Until tomorrow."

Cruising along Starfish Avenue on the island's eastern

side, it took effort to concentrate on the road. I was light as air, only my seatbelt tethering me to earth. My lips were swollen from Jace's kisses—*real* kisses. The sloppy ones by a boorish oaf after a school dance didn't count. I used the pad of my index finger, outlining and lingering over the contours of my lower lip, playing our stolen moments over in my mind. My face flamed. Surely it was stained scarlet. I glimpsed in the rearview. My eyes were bright and sparkling with happiness. Grandmother was too savvy not to notice. Once she learned I was involved with an Upper King boy, there'd be hell to pay.

I passed the parcels of undeveloped prime real estate beyond the lighthouse then came to the turnoff for Shoreside Resort. The building was set away from the road, by the oceanfront, but the fountain centered in the courtyard entry was visible from the gate. Massive and brightly lit, it was a scaled-down version of Rome's Trevi Fountain. A guard shack was beside the locked wrought iron gate, a guard in a butter-yellow uniform waving as I tooled by.

Entering the cottage through the side door, I was dismayed to see the glowing numerals on the microwave display. The hour was far too late. I clicked the deadbolt. In the darkened kitchen, I dropped my sandal in the trash. Lamplight from the parlor spilled into the hall. My grandparents hadn't yet retired to bed. That was unusual.

Oh no. They weren't waiting up for me, were they?

I squared my shoulders, preparing for an onslaught of questions. At the entryway to the parlor, I halted, suddenly sentient of odd energy pulsating through the atmosphere.

Granddad perched on the edge of the settee, hands clasped and head bowed. Grandmother paced the length of the room from the settee to the French doors, her face set in fury. My heart plunged to the floor. Somehow they heard about my moonlight necking session with Jace.

Shit.

"Oh, Kitty Kat," Granddad said mournfully when he spotted me in the entryway. "I'm so sorry…"

CHAPTER SIX

Grandmother whipped around. She scowled at him, her hands balled at her sides. "Confess your misdeeds to your granddaughter, Charles. Confess!"

"I…" Granddad put his palms over his face, a small cry escaping.

"Why should I expect any less of you? You're as weak as water," she sneered. "Shall I tell her then?"

Ignoring Grandmother, I sat beside Granddad and put a hand on his back. "What is it?"

"We just concluded our annual phone conference with Geoffrey," Grandmother informed me. "I've borne your precious grandfather's lies for decades. Every year he vows to amend his conduct… This time, he's finally succeeded in ruining me. This time, there's no recovering!"

Grandmother went to the bookcase and slammed her fist on it. I flinched, my gaze volleying between my grandparents, willing my grandfather to speak.

"Spurning Geoffrey's counsel. Going behind his back. And mine!"

Time slowed as Granddad turned to me, tears wetting his cheeks. "I-I got a tip about some stock while out on the golf course. I figured, why seek advice from Geoffrey or his firm? It was a sure thing. Nobody could've predicted an earthquake would cause the shares to nosedive."

My lips parted. I couldn't comprehend.

"Splashing out for speedboats, private jets, ostentatious jewelry. The losses at the dog track. The failed restaurant ventures," Grandmother hissed. "My ancestors are rolling in their graves. A Randcliffe, destitute?"

"Destitute?" I parroted, numb.

"The house in Boston must be sold. The ranch in Montana. This cottage. Lord, the tongues will be wagging."

Sell Randcliffe Cottage? Light-headed, I put my head between my knees. I'd forgotten how to breathe.

"There are countless debts to satisfy," Grandmother lamented. "I don't know how we'll keep body and soul together. Do you wish to divulge the final nail in the coffin, Charles?"

I sat up abruptly. The room spun as I studied Granddad. He seemed to have shrunk. Looking lost and broken, he met my gaze. "Your trust fund, my dear. It's gone. Your inheritance is gone. Your tuition is gone. It's… all… gone."

"Stayton?" I asked, voice strangled.

Grandmother slumped onto the wing chair beside the settee, deflated and aging before my eyes. "You won't be attending Stayton, Katrina."

Disoriented, and with nothing further to say, we went to bed.

The rhythmic ebb and flow of the ocean waves outside my open bedroom window couldn't console me that night. I tossed and turned until dawn when I drifted into a fitful, nightmare-fueled slumber.

The sun was high in the sky when I woke. Sitting up in bed, I threw off my covers and swung my legs over the side.

Dread lapped at me as I recalled the shocking revelations the night before.

My enrollment at Stayton had been set in stone, my course plotted. Now, my moorings had been severed. My orderly, carefully planned life was thrown into disarray. I was set adrift. Chest compressing, anxiety threatened to overtake me. Now what?

Now what?

I forced myself to draw measured breaths. To control the anxiety. To curb the spiral.

Fresh tears blurred my vision. Snatching a tissue from the box on my bedside table, I swiped them away. I blew my nose then pitched the tattered tissue into the wastebasket by the window.

My grandparents must've risen. Shakily, I twisted my hair into a clip, pulled on a cotton sundress, and stepped into sandals. I was desperate for a crumb of reassurance that everything would be okay, that we'd manage.

The house was silent, Sarah conspicuously absent. I found Grandmother seated beside Granddad at the dining room table. She was hollow-cheeked without makeup, wearing her silk wrap, her hair unbrushed. An uneaten grapefruit half sat on a plate in front of her. She stared at the wall.

Granddad hadn't changed from the clothes he'd worn the day before. In lieu of food, he nursed a Bloody Mary, his eyes red-rimmed and his skin gray. Neither acknowledged my presence.

Finally, Grandmother intoned without emotion, "A visit from a realtor from the mainland is imminent—the cottage will be listed for sale forthwith. Prepare to depart to the city this afternoon."

My gaze skated to Granddad. His chin quivered, but he didn't speak. Lifting his tumbler, he drank.

I slouched into my chair, my stomach queasy, and bit my

fingernails. My brain was muzzy. I had to *do* something! A glance at the clock on the buffet revealed it was eleven.

Jace.

I'd drive to Shoreside and find him. Explain. Give him my contact details, my email address. Get his last name. If I were to leave the island that afternoon, there would be no pizza date.

My grandparents didn't say a word when I got up from my chair and grabbed the car keys from where I'd left them on the kitchen counter. They didn't object when I told them I was going out.

It was a beautifully sunny day, a balmy breeze blowing in from the Atlantic. I drove the ten-minute trip to Shoreside on autopilot, plastering a pleasant expression on my face when I showed my pass at the guard shack.

My palms were wet with perspiration, and moisture beaded on my upper lip. It was taking all I had to act normal. To not surrender to the panic attack I felt rising in my ribcage. Get through this, I told myself as I walked across the parking lot. You can have a meltdown when you come back to the car.

Heart leaping, my eyes locked on Jace from across the expanse of the pool. Golden-skinned and handsome, he was propped casually against the snack bar, bantering with the worker behind the counter. The yellow Speedos with Shoreside's logo Jace wore showed *everything*. He slung the towel he held over a shoulder. His abs rippled.

Despite my current state, I felt a tug of attraction.

My steps faltered when a shapely blonde-haired teenage girl in a brief bikini sidled up to Jace, her arm snaking around his taut midsection. She tipped her head back to say something to him, and they laughed. Nestling her head into his chest, she hugged him. Jace gathered her to him to return the embrace.

They were too intimate with each other. Theirs was not a platonic relationship. Jace obviously wasn't shy about showing affection either—it was bestowed freely and without promises. Tears sprang to my eyes. Why had I read more into our kisses? God, I was stupid. The night before meant nothing to Jace.

Grandmother had told me to never trust silver-tongued townie boys. I should've heeded her advice. Lower King girls were conquests for townies. Mere notches in their bedposts.

Rotating on my heel, I bit down on the fleshy part of my cheek to keep my sobs at bay. I may as well forget Jace.

I had packing to do.

CHAPTER SEVEN

"You're gonna flip your lid!" Fiona exclaimed as she breezed into my office at the Landis-Philips Agency, not pausing to knock. The sunlight slanting through the floor-to-ceiling windows shone on her hair, bringing out the flaxen highlights. She wore an emerald-green jumpsuit, the perfect foil for her coppery curls.

Unperturbed, I sat my coffee cup on my desk, along with my pen. An eyebrow raised in query, I folded my hands and waited for her to take a seat in the chair across from me. It always took Fee forever to get to the point.

"Ran straight in here after I hung up the phone," she wheezed, crossed her legs, then fanned her face. "Phew. Am I out of shape, or what?"

I rolled my eyes. If anyone was out of shape, it was me, from indulging in too much late-night takeout. As a workaholic, I didn't have time to cook or to go to the gym. I'd made peace with the extra twenty pounds I carried. Fee, on the other hand, was rail thin. "You're winded because you only have one speed—fifty miles per hour. Thankfully, you don't wear high heels, or you would've broken an ankle long ago."

She lifted her leg, displaying a metallic-hued ballet flat and shrugging. "Not all of us were made for boring tailored suits with conservative two-inch heels, babe."

I glanced down at my outfit and frowned, mildly offended. What was wrong with my oatmeal-colored linen suit jacket and matching trousers? The frilly shirt I'd chosen was the same pinkish shade as my heels. When I did a fit check in the mirror before leaving my apartment that morning, I thought I looked chic. "I did try."

"I get perverse joy out of teasing you. You're thoroughly presentable, really. That coral blouse is fab with your dark hair." She leaned forward and snagged my cup, guzzling my now room-temperature coffee.

I shook my head at Fee's antics. When I'd met her, her dynamism and brash vivacity jolted my system. She was boisterous and outgoing. I was prudent and reserved. She was the life of the party. I was the wallflower. I'd since grown accustomed to how Fee made a room crackle.

We complemented each other as business partners—Fee inspired me to be bolder, to take risks. In turn, I kept her feet on terra firma when she would otherwise leap too hastily. She tried my patience, but she was my best friend, and I loved her. With a saccharine smile, I drawled, "Thank you, Coco Chanel. Your approbation means everything to me. Now, what's this about a phone call?"

Fee set the empty coffee cup on my desk. "It was Sandra calling from Coast Realty."

I straightened in my seat. Cassandra "Sandra" Daniels was a connection I'd made through a client. She worked at a brokerage in South Carolina. On my behalf, Sandra had approached the current owner of Randcliffe Cottage several times through the years, inquiring whether he could be persuaded to sell. He'd steadfastly flouted my offers, no matter how generous they were.

"I knew that would get your motor revving seeing how single-minded you've been to get the property back."

My mouth was dry. I swallowed. "Why didn't she call me?"

"She did, but it went straight to voicemail. Since it was urgent, Sandra tried me."

"Urgent?" I asked.

"The cottage is coming up for auction on Friday."

"Not this Friday? As in two days from now?"

"Yeah."

"But, why auction?" I ran my fingers through my hair, causing strands to escape my chignon. "That doesn't make sense."

Fee relaxed against the chair cushion. "Been a while since Sandra contacted the owner, hasn't it?"

I nodded. "Over a year now. When she last touched base with him, he was combative, so I told her we better cool it. Apparently," I hesitated, trying to be charitable, "he was a difficult man. An eccentric man."

"He died in the interim, and his heirs must not have been aware of your offers. They let 'acquaintances' stay there and —get this—they didn't even draw up a lease. According to Sandra, the people weren't Lower Kingfisher standard either."

I whistled, my thoughts racing. "I'm sure the high-pedigreed neighbors weren't happy. That section of the island is too bougie for commoners. Let me guess… the acquaintances quit paying their rent and the property went into foreclosure, hence the auction."

"You've got it in one. The heirs had it mortgaged to the hilt. The renters squatted there through the winter. Thing is, Kit…"

Something in Fee's expression made my stomach drop. "Oh, no. What is it?"

"Sandra drove over and peered in the windows?" Fee clicked her tongue. "It's rough. Hoarding rough."

Sentimentality had my nose dripping and eyes watering. Randcliffe Cottage had once been a fine home. A grand old lady. The thought of her being disrespected—cast aside as if she were rubbish—was a heartbreaking prospect. I coughed away the tightness in my throat and opened my desk drawer, extracting a tissue. "Traveling to Kingfisher Cove now isn't feasible. I'm *so* close to pinning the Sumans down. We're viewing the Vista la Montana house Friday. I expect them to bite."

"That place is a dinosaur and overpriced to boot. You and I both know the listing agent's comps were out of whack. You really think you can move it?"

"I persuaded the owners to have the interior painted last week, then I hired a staging company."

"You're footing the bill for the stagers? Shut up! That must've cost the moon."

"It wasn't cheap," I conceded. "But it's worth the gamble."

Fee's gaze was canny. "Not like you to gamble."

"After all the showings and not a nibble from them, I'm running out of options. With the commission, I can afford to take the summer off. It'd be enough time to fix up the cottage."

"Why not have Jeanine or Mick show it to the Sumans instead? That way you can fly out to the Cove tomorrow."

"No, they want me. An associate isn't good enough." I narrowed my eyes at Fee. "Any chance *you'd* be my proxy at the auction?"

CHAPTER EIGHT

CHARLENE SUMAN SHIFTED HER YORKIE FROM ONE ARM TO THE other and clapped her hands. A labradoodle at her heels barked. "Murray-kins, look! Did you count the bedrooms? There are enough for all the babies to each have their own."

Murray intoned around the toothpick in his mouth, "They sleep with us in our bed every night anyhow, dumplin' pie."

I was certain playing into my clients' love for their canines would be my saving grace—they owned a string of dog kibble manufacturing plants, and their pets were their kids. One wouldn't know by the Sumans' appearance that they were billionaires. They were in their sixties, their wardrobe straight from a clearance bin at a discount store. Murray wore a striped shirt with elastic around the waistline and polyester pants, a baseball cap on his head. Charlene's colorful muumuu was paired with crepe-soled orthopedic sneakers.

I bit my lip, my faith flagging. Would all the expense of staging be for naught?

Murray scratched the jowls of the tubby chiweenie he held, then he placed it on the floor. The dog waddled to the corner of the bedroom where there was a decorative fire hydrant, lifting a leg to piddle. I cringed, stifling the urge to run to the kitchen for paper towels and disinfectant spray to scrub the outdated yet immaculate travertine tiles.

Murray's shrewd gaze roamed over the coved ceilings and Venetian plastered walls. The framed portraits of dogs wearing Renaissance-style clothes and hats with feather plumes caught his eye. He steepled his stubby fingers. "Hmm."

Charlene's yorkie yipped. "Do you want down too, Snuggies? Go have fun with YumYum and Tootles, baby boy."

Snuggies chased YumYum the labradoodle, and Tootles the chiweenie joined in, weaving around Charlene and Murray's ankles. Charlene clung to Murray's forearm as the dogs rocketed into her.

It was pandemonium.

Pinching the bridge of my nose, I prayed for strength. After all the showings the last three months with the Sumans and their menagerie, I was at the end of my tether.

Bending to pick up a chew toy from a woven basket by an oversized dog bed, I schooled my face blank. Fee was in Kingfisher Cove, and the auction for the cottage had already begun. I was dying to know what was happening. Sidestepping over to the maltipoo puppy gnawing at the doorframe trim, I shook the knotted rope, sing-songing, "Do you want the toy?"

YumYum broke away from the pack, almost toppling Murray. He bore down on me, his tongue lolling. Suppressing a squeak, I chucked the toy across the room. YumYum skidded, changed direction, and bounded after it, the maltipoo puppy in pursuit.

I beamed at Charlene, brushing at the dirty paw prints the labradoodle had left on my trousers earlier when he'd jumped on me while I wrestled with the front door lockbox.

"Kitty," Charlene enthused, "I know my Murray-kins is balking at the price, but this house is utter perfection."

My cell rang. I apologized to the Sumans, peeking at the

display. It was Fee. "I must take this call. Pardon me." I stepped out to the hall, answering with, "Tell me good news."

"Bidding war. Ten grand over your max," Fee said hurriedly. "What do you want me to do?"

My palms drenched with sweat. Randcliffe Cottage was tantalizingly within my grasp. If it meant digging deep into my pockets, so be it. I couldn't lose. "I have the funds. Go for it."

"FYI, we couldn't go inside, but I looked in the windows. Sandra's right. It's bad."

"I don't care." I named an amount she could bid up to. With a shocked gasp, Fee ended the call. I stepped back into the bedroom with the Sumans—the pressure was on. It was vital this sale closed today. "I saved the best for last. Please come with me."

I sent up a prayer that Murray would be seduced by the staging company's décor in the basketball court. I was pleased they'd followed my instructions to a T otherwise, filling the house with dog-friendly furniture. However, the gym was my *pièce de résistance*. The clincher.

When I got to the door at the end of the hallway, Tootles leaped on my leg. I bumped into the wall. "Ack!"

"Sorry, Kitty. He's booked in for a neuter Thursday." Charlene chastised Tootles as she stooped to pluck him off me, "No, no, baby. We don't hump our realtor."

I flashed an awkward smile, recovering enough to open the door. "The indoor gymnasium."

The dogs ran into the space, sniffing the trampoline, the tunnels and playhouses, and the plastic pool filled with balls. Charlene gasped, "It's like doggy daycare!"

Murray stood in the center of the gym, observing his dogs frolic, his beefy hands on his hips.

Charlene went to her husband, threading her arm through his and simpering up at him. "What do you say, Murray-kins?

They don't make houses like this one anymore—it's my dream home."

He sighed, saying, "Alrighty, dumplin' pie."

The staging had worked.

A self-satisfied zip I felt was the thrill of victory laced with relief. From the periphery, YumYum galloped toward me. I braced for impact, and the labradoodle sprang up, his front paws planting on my shoulders. Sagging under his weight, I grappled to hold him, and he licked my face. I threw my head back, angling out of his reach.

"Aww, mama's wittle Yummy thinks he's a lapdog," Charlene crooned in baby talk. "He woves you, Kitty."

I laughed to cover my discomfiture. The heel on one of my pumps snapped off, and I teetered, losing my balance. The kiddie playhouse beside me broke my fall. YumYum landed with all four paws on the floor, then, rebounding, went to pursue Snuggies through the tunnel system, no worse for the wear. I used the sleeve of my fitted blazer to wipe slobber from my face. Smoothing a hank of hair that had come out of my bun, I found it soaked. Yuck. Withholding a shudder and teeth gritted, I wiped my palm on my trousers.

"Let's head back to Kitty's office and put in an offer," Murray told Charlene then fixed his attention to me, resituating the toothpick he had in his mouth. "The dog stuff is included in the price, right?"

CHAPTER NINE

My cell pinged on the drive to Landis-Phillips, alerting me of a voicemail. I glimpsed covertly at the display. Fee. Was I the highest bidder?

Armpits damp from nerves, I wrote up the Sumans' offer. After fifteen minutes of tense negotiation, to my utter relief, the seller accepted Murray's terms. With the inspection scheduled the following week, we shook hands across my desk, and the Sumans took their leave.

At last, I was free to hear the news.

My heartbeat flapped in my sternum like birds' wings, making me jittery and breathless as I listened to Fee's message. The bidding war jacked the price up, but I came out on top. Randcliffe Cottage was mine. My penny-pinching ways—and my forthcoming commission—assured I could shoulder the cost. Nevertheless, the price tag stung. Ouch.

Before signing off, Fee demanded, "Call me, babe."

I won. The. Cottage. Was. Mine. I now had a seaside refuge of my very own.

My plans were finally coming to fruition. Years had been spent scrimping and saving for the day I had the opportunity to buy the home, to return her to the family.

In my daydreams, I'd often fantasized about choosing linens and wallcoverings. Hunting for décor on the mainland. Whiling away lazy June afternoons on the front veranda, where I'd sip lemonade and read a novel.

What was strange was that I expected to feel a jolt of triumph upon hearing I won the auction. Instead, I was engulfed by a curious emotion I couldn't identify—a combination of anxiety, self-doubt, and melancholy.

Memories bubbled up. Hazy, halcyon. Mostly pleasant. Splashing in the Atlantic with my nanny. The salt on my skin drying to crust in the mid-day sun as we ate finger sandwiches. My feet in powdery sand. Sweet-smelling Carolina jessamine dripping off the vine. Granddad treating me to ice cream after tennis lessons at Shoreside. Hollby Lighthouse, where the handsome lifeguard—Jace—saved me from tumbling into the surf. Our shared confidences at sunset, the air rife with excitement. Possibility. Then that terrible night when my world came crashing to the ground. The added insult of seeing my love interest cozying up with another girl. How I'd lost him before he was mine.

"No. Not going there." Shaking my head, I straightened up my desk, typed out an email, and poured a glass of Chablis before dialing Fee.

She picked up on the second ring. "Congrats, homeowner."

I exhaled, took a sip of wine, and leaned back in my chair. "Thanks."

"How're you doing?"

"I'm reeling," I admitted with a short laugh.

"You've been so intent on getting the property back for so long, it's probably a mindfuck to finally have it."

"It is." I told Fee about the la Montana sale, explaining Murray Suman's push for a speedy closing. "Mick will handle it while I'm at the Cove."

Together, we chorused, "Perk of being the boss."

"You've had quite the day," Fee noted.

"Yes, I have."

"What was the Sumans' record? Ninety-four houses?"

I snorted. "I showed them and their crazy pack of mutts one hundred seven houses, including la Montana."

"You deserve a medal! We'll celebrate when you arrive at Kingfisher Cove. Are you flying out tomorrow?"

"Hopefully. I have to buy a ticket. I've already sent out a company-wide email to inform everyone I'll only be available remotely 'til August."

"I saw that. Plenty of jaws fell to the floor reading it, I imagine. Kitty Landis actually taking a vacation! Wonders never cease." Fee paused, her manner turning serious. "Brace yourself. I'm about to text interior photos of the cottage."

I put Fee on speakerphone. A minute later, six images came through. Swallowing hard, I enlarged one taken of the parlor, attempting to look past the heaped detritus, filth, and abandoned furniture to the bones of the room. The built-ins were destroyed as if someone had taken an ax to them, the walls buckling from age. Scrolling the photos, I found the dining room windows broken, covered with cardboard and duct tape. Both the kitchen and the hall bathroom were anni-hilated, gaping holes in the walls, cabinets smashed, and fixtures missing. I'd been warned the cottage was in bad shape, but I hadn't foreseen *this*.

Eyes flooding with tears, I cleared my throat, not wanting Fee to detect how distraught I was. She did anyway.

"Makes your hovel seem like a villa in comparison, doesn't it?"

The hovel Fee referred to was the poky efficiency apart-ment on the outskirts of Santa Beatriz we'd leased together while building our empire a decade earlier. Fee had since moved on, purchasing a swanky condo by the beach once we started making real money. I was more frugal, the allure of cheap rent rooting me in place. "The squatters really did a number on it... what's with the holes in the walls?"

"They harvested the copper. Sooo, major plumbing work is in order."

Fingertips kneading my temples, I asked, "Water damage?"

"Shut off before they tore the copper out, fortunately. *Un*fortunately, they must've penned animals in the primary bedroom. It reeks. Electrical looks functional but since the power's off, I can't check. Besides which, they stole all the light fixtures."

"They were original to the house. It'll cost a small fortune to replace them." Great. Wisps of panic crept into my chest. I downed the remainder of my Chablis. "Did I make a mistake?"

Fee clucked, softening. "You're overwhelmed right now, but you've got the resources to restore the cottage to its former glory. And although I can't hang around to help you, Sandra knows people. She's chummy with the owners of a general contracting firm. Atlas something. Highly recommends them. Do you want me to set up an appointment for them to come over for a look? She said to mention her name, and they'd give you priority."

———

SATURDAY AFTERNOON, I landed in Georgia, renting a car at the airport for the drive to Kingfisher Cove. It was a sunny, seasonal day, but I was knotted inside out.

I opened the windows and gulped the fresh breeze. In a rush of bravado, I cranked the volume on the radio and sang along to nineties pop. I was on vacation and should act like it, dammit. To relax for once. To live in the moment. It was too easy to dwell on the litany of tasks that lay ahead of me and spiral. First, I'd check into the hotel. Then, I'd join

Fee. She'd scored me a room adjacent to hers at Shoreside Resort.

At the turnoff for the parkway bridge, I silenced the radio, my heart accelerating with anticipation now that I was closing in on my destination. It had been fifteen years since I'd been there, and I wanted to see how much it had changed.

The mainland behind me, Silber Sound was to my right, appearing just as I remembered it. Cleary Beach was in the distance, scattered with hardy beachgoers who didn't seem daunted by the chilly May water temperature. On the left of the parkway, the harbor teemed with activity, seagulls circling the fishing boats returning with their wares. Horns from the crafts signaled their entry into the marina.

Muscle memory kicked in at the intersection at the base of the bridge. Rather than take Starfish Avenue, which wove around the island, I opted for a shortcut through the land-locked residential section in Mid-King which was crammed with rental properties.

Shoreside's guard shack was gone, the gates pulled back to allow unfettered access to the resort. I tooled down the macadam lane and around the sparkling fountain. At the curb in front of the resort proper, I wondered if valet parking was a thing of yesteryear, like the guard shack, but workers in butter-yellow polo shirts and pressed khakis materialized within seconds. A pair of porters took custody of my luggage as the valet attendant parked my rental.

"This way, madam," a uniformed doorman said, holding the door for me. He swept me into the lobby, where I stopped short.

I took in the airy atrium, dazed. The furniture was now upholstered in navy and cream stripes, but the vintage wallpaper festooned with whimsical sea creatures remained. A cluster of smartly dressed guests gathered in conversation at the bottom of the grand stairway. I was drawn to the framed photo display on the wall behind them. Murmuring a perfunctory "Excuse me," I veered around them as if no longer in control of my body.

A peculiar sense of déjà vu hit me. We Randcliffes were all in attendance, immortalized there in black and white. I sought out the newer photos—my mother in a floor-length gown, posing with other debutantes. My grandparents at a New Year's Eve party, Grandmother in a matronly drop-waisted dress and Granddad in a natty tux. Grandmother, Granddad, and me in a candid snap during a golf game my seventeenth visit to the island.

If only that endearingly insecure, naïve girl could know how drastically her life would be altered her eighteenth year, she wouldn't have smiled as brightly.

CHAPTER TEN

SHOWERED AND DRESSED IN A SLEEVELESS BLOUSE, CRISP trousers, and espadrilles, I met Fee at The Seafarer, the laid-back eatery on Shoreside's grounds.

Preferring to be by the water, we lounged at the outdoor bar, the sun on our backs. We snacked on canapés, drinking cosmos and chatting. Using a napkin, I sketched a layout of the cottage's kitchen, and we discussed cabinetry and countertop options. While Fee flirted with the bartender, a mother and her toddler collecting seashells on the beach snagged my eye. Had my mom ever done that with me? She must've, but I was too young when she died to recall.

The bartender moved on to serve other patrons, and Fee swiveled in her seat. She smiled as the toddler kneeled to examine a piece of driftwood, his face screwed up in concentration. "Cute."

My gaze slid to her. An afternoon decompressing with my BFF was what the doctor ordered. The two cosmos helped, too. I settled back in my rattan barstool and let out a leisurely breath. "I love it here."

"Tell me about it. I had the most amazing massage at the spa this morning." Fee pointed to the stylish printed romper she wore. "I bought this in the shop afterward. They have killer dresses. Want to pop in and pick one up before we head over to the cottage?"

"I meant I love Kingfisher Cove," I said, "and the last thing I should do is drop five hundred clams on a designer sundress—my pocketbook is already steaming, and I haven't even gotten quotes for the work that needs to be done!"

"You look like you're about to attend a realtor's association dinner in those slacks. A sundress ain't gonna break you, babe, not with the way you economize." She requested our bill. "If only I had your willpower when it comes to money."

I lifted a brow. "I noticed the bracelet and the sandals."

Fee grinned as she signed for the tab, charging everything to her room. "I decided to live a little."

"You're gonna 'live a little' yourself into the poorhouse," I cautioned.

With an insouciant shrug, Fee slipped from her stool and grabbed her clutch. "I'll sell that commercial warehouse on Via Verde when I get back to Santa Beatriz to make up for it. Either that or marry a billionaire."

I snorted then suggested, "Let's run over to the cottage before the sun sets."

We walked back to the hotel on the clamshell footpath, waiting while her rental was fetched from valet parking. The attendant pulled up in a flashy sports car. When we settled into the low-slung vehicle, I clicked my seatbelt, shooting Fee an amused look. "Want to guess what I rented?"

"A sensible mid-size sedan?"

"Bingo."

We shared a laugh as Fee zipped down the lane.

HANDS CLENCHED IN MY LAP, I assessed the damage as Fee parked in the driveway. A couple broken windows.

Chipped paint on the siding. A weed-choked yard. Fee switched off the ignition and dug in her clutch for the house keys. I exited the car, saying, "Not as awful as I anticipated."

"Wait 'til you see inside." She gestured to the bundled newspapers piled near the curb. "Why didn't the owners cancel their subscription?"

I pictured Granddad poring over *The Cove Observer* at the breakfast table. "It's a free weekly publication with community news. Every residence on the island receives it."

"Do people read newspapers anymore?" Fee scoffed before ceremoniously handing me the keys to the cottage. I gagged as I entered the kitchen. There was a window above where the sink had been. Picking around the trash on the floor, Fee unlatched it and pushed up the sash. "You can't say I didn't warn you. I'll let you check things out while I go around and open the rest of the windows."

Cell in hand, I typed notes. Windows. Plumbing. Electrical. Flooring, drywall, and lighting. In the parlor, I kicked aside cereal boxes and a stack of dirty clothes in my path. The windows in the French doors were covered with cobwebs, but the doors were operational. I added built-ins and paint to my list.

Fee strode down the hall as I went to inspect the bathroom there, a sharp stench wafting after her. She pinched her nose with her fingers, her voice nasally when she explained, "The bedroom door was shut to contain the fumes."

I blanched, holding my index finger under my nostrils. "Oof."

"Funnily enough, the en suite bathroom is virtually untouched."

We poked our heads in the hallway bathroom before continuing to the bedrooms. I said, "Total gut."

"Yep."

My old bedroom was a hoarder's paradise, but the condition of the primary bedroom was unspeakable. Nose wrinkling, I groaned. "This is a shovel-required situation."

"Once it's cleared out, the general smell should improve."

We went outdoors, strolling past Fee's rental to the overgrown backyard where the vegetation grew unchecked and unrestrained. Fifty yards from the crumbling paver patio behind the house, water lapped the sandy shore, the briny scent serving as a palate cleanser. Standing shoulder to shoulder, we inhaled lungfuls of air and surveyed the majesty of the Atlantic Ocean, which stretched as far as the eye could see. I asked, "What's the name of that company Sandra recommended?"

"Atlas All Trades. An Ethan Atlas will be here noon tomorrow."

"Wow." My eyebrows raised, I gave Fee a look. "On a *Sunday*?"

"Sandra's name has pull."

The breeze blew tendrils of hair in my face. I tucked them behind my ear, my mood contemplative. "I hope they can begin work right away. What if I can't get the cottage livable by the end of the summer?"

"It'd be tough managing a project of this scope from the west coast," Fee assented, "but what's the hurry?"

"There isn't one. Not really. It's just that I'd love to fly out for Christmas on the island." I'd loop evergreen garlands over the parlor built-ins, put a tree with Napco ornaments in the corner.

"Well. It is the off-season so... maybe." Fee hitched a hip, putting her hand on it and scolding, "You've waited years for this moment, Kit. Enjoy the process, for crying out loud. You've earned it."

She was right, of course. "I need to remind myself."

"Yes, you do," Fee said pertly, then asked, "Am I to receive an invitation next summer?"

"You can count on that," I promised, feeling a swell of

gratitude for my friend. My throat tight, I faced Fee. "Thank you for coming out here. For bidding on the cottage for me."

Unconcerned, she said, "You bankrolled the trip. I would've been a fool to decline a gratis vacation."

"When's your flight home?"

"Tomorrow afternoon."

"Oh, good. We can have brunch together at Shoreside."

Fee nodded. "Do you want me to tag along to your appointment here? I can drive separately and go straight to the airport afterward."

"Yes, please."

We meandered the perimeter of the property, reaching the driveway. Deciding it would be acceptable to leave the windows ajar overnight, I bolted the kitchen door.

The sun began its descent on the ten-minute journey back to the resort. My mind felt cluttered, but I was calm, centered. The list of tasks I'd typed out on my phone meant I had a game plan in place. Once I returned to my room, I'd take out my laptop and get to work researching light fixtures and décor.

Turning onto Shoreside's macadam lane, Fee remarked in a mischievous way, "I know that expression on your face. Your confidence has rallied—you're a woman on a mission."

CHAPTER ELEVEN

A BLUE AND WHITE VAN DECORATED WITH THE OUTLINE OF A figure holding a globe on his shoulders was in the driveway when we arrived at the cottage at quarter to twelve Sunday. Fee followed me from Shoreside, parking her rental behind mine at the curb.

"A punctual contractor," she quipped as we picked across the rutted front yard on the hunt for Ethan Atlas, sidestepping an aluminum ladder. "What a novelty."

A muscular man around our age—early thirties—wearing a T-shirt and jeans was on his hands and knees in the backyard, scrutinizing the cottage's foundation. Fee elbowed me, a suggestive gleam in her eye.

When the man saw us, he smiled and got up, dusting his palms on his backside.

"Kitty Landis?"

"I'm Kitty." I took the calloused hand he presented and shook it. He was cute, boyish.

"Ethan Atlas. Nice to meet you."

"This is my friend, Fiona Phillips."

"Right. Fiona. We spoke on the phone," Ethan said.

"We sure did." They shook hands, and Fee batted her

eyelashes up at him, unmistakably smitten. I could see Ethan's appeal—he was tall, with bronzed skin and hazel eyes which crinkled at the corners when he smiled.

Fee glanced between me and Ethan, her gaze narrowing as she zeroed in on his ring finger. Oh, crap. She was plotting how to play matchmaker. *Not today, Cupid*. I veered the subject back to the cottage, thanking Ethan for coming over on a Sunday. "How does the foundation look?"

"Solid. Porch is, too. I've already been on the roof, and I don't see issues with that either. Windows... you don't want new ones, do you?"

"Heavens, no," I protested. "They're original to the cottage and the frames are pristine. I thought we'd replace the panes... reglaze the glass or whatever?"

"Fiona mentioned your intent for restoration rather than modernization." Judging by Ethan's expression, I could tell he approved.

We made our way to the front of the cottage. Ethan braced a booted foot on the veranda step then ran a hand through his dirty-blond hair, squinting as he surveyed the property. "A lick of paint. Landscaping. Re-lay the paver patio out back. Maybe add wisteria on a trellis."

Fee chimed in, "How about cedar boxes under the windows?"

I'd imagined the yard filled with a profusion of flowers. "Yes, and I'd love a pergola over the driveway vined with Carolina jessamine."

"There's one out back you can transplant, isn't there?" she asked.

I nodded, turning to Ethan. "So any exterior work is purely cosmetic?"

"Right."

Taking the house keys from my purse, I replied, "The interior's a different story. Shall we?"

Ethan picked up a clipboard from the ground beside the

ladder then motioned us forward with an affable grin. "Lead the way, Ms. Landis, Ms. Phillips."

I instinctively returned his grin, climbing the veranda stairs to unlock the front door. Sandra's recommendation carried a lot of weight, but my gut told me Ethan was a decent sort. Trustworthy. As Fee and I showed him around the cottage, he was all business, penciling notes on the notepad attached to his clipboard. I described my vision—refurbished built-ins, period light fixtures, and hardwood flooring. I got the impression Ethan was someone who valued old homes like I did. My relief was palpable—so many people preferred to rip out what gave character and replace with the latest trendy materials. I mentally crossed my fingers that Atlas would be able to take on the job.

Ethan whistled when we reached the primary bedroom.

"As you can see, leaving the windows open," I grimaced, "didn't help much."

Nose pinched, Fee retreated. "I hope the hardwoods under the carpet aren't spoiled."

"No," I replied, "there aren't wood floors in the bedrooms, although I do want some installed."

"The waste might have soaked into the subfloor. We won't know 'til the carpet and padding are ripped out," Ethan warned.

We ended the tour in the kitchen, where he evaluated the breaker box in the pantry. "I'm a licensed electrician. The wiring's outdated but appears sound. Tomorrow you can phone Island Power and request they reconnect you."

"I'll do that." Preparing myself for an astronomical figure, I asked, "Can you give me a hint what the project will cost?"

Ethan consulted his clipboard then threw out a number less than I expected. "I'll write up an itemized estimate and get it to you by mid-week at the latest."

"When can you start work?"

"Early June? We have a big job by Cleary Beach we're

wrapping up and another on deck, but we can squeeze you in. Our summer schedule fills fast, so it's fortunate Fiona called when she did." Securing his pencil under the fastener, Ethan tucked the clipboard under his arm.

Fee fished in her clutch for her cell, peeping at the display. To make her flight, she must leave by one. Bestowing a bright smile on Ethan, she wheedled, "There's no way you can get the cottage on your schedule a smidge earlier? Kitty's living out of a suitcase at Shoreside right now."

"I'll see what I can do," he promised.

"How long will it take to make the cottage livable?" I asked swiftly before Fee did something like insinuate Ethan take me to dinner. "I'd rather stay here, even if I have to use a sleeping bag."

"Depends on how long it takes to remove the garbage and get you running water." Ethan paused, perusing me as if he were sizing me up. "You know, if you're interested in speeding the process, there is something you *can* do…"

"Yes?" I prompted.

"If you're amenable, I can arrange dumpster delivery from the mainland tomorrow, and you can empty the house yourself. That way my men can begin the more important jobs straightaway."

I blew a raspberry, considering. I'd rather jump in front of a speeding locomotive than deal with the waste in the primary bedroom, but it wasn't like I had anything else better to do. "Okay. I'm game for some sweat equity. Bring it on."

Ethan assured me he'd drop the estimate by ASAP so we could formalize our agreement. Fee and I followed him out, and he gave me a business card before shaking hands with us. After loading the ladder on his truck, he bid us farewell.

We waved as Ethan reversed out of the driveway. Fee grumbled, "You should treat him to a drink at The Seafarer. He's not wearing a ring."

"Ha! You think you're pretty slick, but I guessed what you were up to."

"Nothing wrong with mixing business with pleasure," Fee sniffed.

"He is handsome... but there's no time for that now. I have to shovel out the entire cottage." I gave her a rueful look. "You sure I can't persuade you to stay this week and assist me with the clean out?"

Fee laughed and laughed.

CHAPTER TWELVE

THE DUMPSTER WAS DROPPED OFF AT THE COTTAGE AT NOON ON Monday. I'd spent the morning shopping on the mainland for supplies before grabbing a sandwich. After dining cross-legged on the paver patio, I unloaded my parcels from my rental, raring to get my hands dirty.

I set the plastic bin in the center of the bedroom and flung open the French doors overlooking the expanse of backyard and the ocean. Gloved and masked, I began shoveling. It was nasty work. Even with the breeze coming off the water, the ammonia odor from the carpet stung my eyes, and I had to step outside frequently. When the bin was full, I dragged it through the doors, across the patio, and around the house to the dumpster in the driveway. Then I repeated the process.

Island Power hadn't yet reconnected the electricity, so the waning afternoon light halted my workday. Sweaty and stinky and my overalls stained with muck, I shed my gloves and yanked off my mask. I propped against the back of the house to catch my breath, feeling filthy and exhausted but accomplished.

The piles of excrement had been removed from the bedroom. I planned to tear out the carpet tomorrow. The walls were in desperate need of washing, but without water in the cottage, there wasn't much cleaning I could do.

"Yoo hoo!" a voice boomed from the distance.

I started, combing the backyards to my left.

"I'm here!"

I wheeled to my right. A slight-framed, elderly woman sat in a wicker rocker two cottages away. She wore periwinkle pajamas that matched the hue of her hair. Raising an arm, she beckoned me over.

How could I refuse joining her? I crossed my fingers that she wasn't downwind of me as I approached her. I didn't exactly smell like roses.

The woman was easily in her late nineties. Though her face was lined with age, her eyes were sharp. A walker was on one side of her chair, an end table on the other. A copy of *The Cove Observer* and a pair of bejeweled spectacles rested on the table. "Good evening. I'm Mitzi Armbruster."

"Pleasure to meet you," I replied. "I'm Kitty Landis, the owner of Randcliffe Cottage."

A middle-aged brunette dressed in rainbow patterned scrubs stepped from the house carrying a highball glass filled to the brim with purplish liquid on the rocks. "Why, hello there. I didn't realize Ms. Mitzi had company. Can I mix you a Mauve Madness, too?"

I began, "I shouldn't—"

"Of course you should! It's my signature cocktail," Mitzi said. "Brenda, a seat for my guest, please."

"Sure thing, Ms. Mitzi." Brenda passed her the drink before turning to fetch a chair.

I put my palms up. "No, I can't stay—"

"You must," Mitzi declared, her voice strident. I couldn't stop staring at her eyes—she had Elizabeth Taylor eyes. The periwinkle pajamas brought out their violet tones, making them all the more dramatic. "It took Brenda practice, but now she whips up a mean cocktail."

Brenda brought another rocker from the covered carport attached to the house—a dwelling similar to my cottage but with weathered wood shingles rather than siding. "Here you are, miss. I'll be back in a jiff with your drink."

She disappeared inside, leaving us alone. Mitzi indicated the rocker with a heavily veined hand. Rays from the sun setting over the water sparked the amethysts on the rings she wore. "Take a load off, doll."

I perched on the edge of the seat. "I'm such a mess. I ought to—"

"Pfft. Pay that no mind." The ice in Mitzi's cocktail clinked as she drank it. She smacked her lips before setting the glass on her side table. "Refreshing as ever. I have to tell you, I was over the moon when the Randcliffe place sold. Those last renters were horrid."

"That's what I heard. They certainly left the cottage in shambles."

Mitzi squinted at me then slipped on her spectacles. "Kitty Landis, you say? Landis. Hmmm."

Alarm bells clanged as Mitzi gave me a painstaking once over. When Brenda emerged from the house with my cocktail, I seized the opportunity to avoid replying to Mitzi.

"Why don't I prepare your dinner while you visit with your new neighbor?"

"Brilliant idea." After the screen door slammed behind Brenda, Mitzi told me, "I know who you are."

My stomach dropped. I wasn't prepared for anyone to recognize me on the island—I should have prepared. Busying myself with my drink, I took a mouthful and swallowed slowly. It was a delicious libation, comprised of gin, pomegranate juice, and grapefruit seltzer. "Oh?"

Mitzi tsked. "You're Helena's girl. There's no denying that —you're a Randcliffe through and through."

My gaze cut to hers. There wasn't any malice there, only curiosity. Intuition told me Mitzi was harmless. And she spoke the truth. There was no use denying my lineage. The Randcliffe genes were strong. Still, I wasn't sure how to respond.

"What's the subterfuge about, doll?"

I sidestepped her query about why I didn't use my given name, shrugging. "I didn't expect anyone to know who I was, that's all. It threw me. You knew my family?"

"Oh, yes. We ran in the same circles, though I had a couple years on your grandmother. This place was built by my husband Anson's people, you see. I escaped to the Cove to grieve after he croaked—it was a great consolation for me— and I never left again."

Now that the cat was out of the bag about my identity, it was like a weight had been eased from my shoulders. I relaxed into the rocker, smiling at Mitzi and thinking how her bouffant hairstyle, vibrant silk pajamas, and marabou slippers suited her personality. "I can't believe I don't remember you. You're a person not easily forgotten."

"Indeed not!" Mitzi laughed uproariously then coughed, her slight body wracking. I straightened in concern, but she motioned me away. By the time she caught her air, her complexion was florid. She picked up her cocktail and took a swig. "My health has always been precarious. I'm appalled that I've outlived my contemporaries."

I liked Mitzi Armbruster—she was a character—and what a treat it was to encounter someone who had known my family during the good times. "You said you socialized with my grandparents?"

"To be frank, I was never accepted into Frances's inner circle. I always stood out from the crowd with my loud lavender outfits, my dyed hair, and my penchant for vulgar jewelry. I was outspoken for the era, too unconventional. Plus, my father wasn't a steel magnate or an oil tycoon. He owned a lowly hardware store, you see. She was a bit of a snob, old Frances. Insufferable with it, at times."

That last tidbit was imparted with no rancor, only brutal honesty. Now it was my turn to laugh. "Yes, she was sometimes."

"I got on with Charlie, naturally. He was a man's man. Bit of a chancer, though. Rather fond of the dog track, was Charlie."

I nodded. Swirling the grapefruit wedge in my cocktail with the stirrer, I opted to take the bull by the horns. "So you must recall my family's inauspicious departure from Kingfisher Cove?"

Mitzi tilted her head, her gaze thoughtful. "Is that stuck in your craw? The humiliation of the mighty Randcliffes' diminished social station?"

Not answering at first, I instead focused on a pair of Belted Kingfishers near the shoreline. "I don't know if I'd put it that way, but there is a measure of humiliation with how things went down," I conceded.

"But that's par for the course among the wealthy set, doll," Mitzi said breezily. "Fortunes are attained, fortunes are frittered. *C'est la vie.*"

"Perhaps. I know my grandmother was greatly affronted by losing hers."

"Well, her identity was centered around being an heiress." Mitzi rolled her eyes heavenward. "Frances delighted in lording her ancestry over others on a regular basis. She irritated me. I told her so to her face once. She wasn't best pleased. Not that I cared."

"Goodness." A scandalized giggle burbled out of me. "There's no love lost there, huh, Mitzi?"

Mitzi grinned, displaying ill-fitting dentures. "I told you I'm too outspoken. I didn't dislike Frances. Don't believe that. It's only that she had a superiority complex, you see. She was nauseatingly smug about her family name. I simply couldn't relate to her."

"Neither could I," I admitted softly. "She was complicated

and overbearing and self-important. Nevertheless, I loved her."

"Why, of course you did. That's patently obvious," Mitzi said. "Yet I sense you wish to remain incognito while on island."

My throat clogged with emotion. "Not being Katrina Randcliffe... it allows me a fresh start, you know? One not saddled with what happened in the past."

Mitzi tapped an index finger against the side of her nose. "I'll take it to my grave, doll."

After I thanked her for understanding, we lapsed into silence, listening to the waves break the shore as the sun disappeared into the sea. I finished my now watery cocktail. When Mitzi again turned to me, her winsome expression was at odds with her forceful personality. "Sometimes it's too quiet here, particularly in the off-season. When I'm too unwell to leave my bed, I have Brenda, but she's paid to be here... I do hope we can be friends, Kitty."

Touched, I put my empty glass on the table and leaned over to pat her hand. "I hope so, too."

The screen door creaked open, and Brenda stepped outside. "I didn't want to interrupt, but Ms. Mitzi's dinner's getting cold."

It was growing late. Twilight had settled over the backyard.

"Brenda, can you assist me? I'm afraid I'm feeling rather weary." As Brenda came across the lawn, Mitzi told me, "It's hell getting old, Kitty. I don't recommend it. Say, care to join me for dinner?"

I felt a twinge of contrition—I'd overstayed. How had I missed the signs that Mitzi was flagging? "Not tonight. Maybe another time."

As I left, Mitzi called, "Don't be a stranger now."

I promised I'd visit again soon, then I went back to my cottage, my mind on Mitzi Armbruster and the information she had about my family. I was eager to get better acquainted with her.

My phone was on the patio, the display showing a text from Fee. I answered her before going inside and stripping down. Loath to shock Shoreside's staff with my unkempt appearance, I dressed in the slacks and blouse I'd brought along.

After locking up and pitching my overalls in the dumpster, I drove to the resort, yawning and my stomach growling. While waiting for my room service order, I showered, noting the soreness in my back and shoulders. Unaccustomed to manual labor, my body begged for rest.

Immediately after eating, I tumbled into bed.

CHAPTER THIRTEEN

Over the next days, I developed a routine. Rise early, eat a light breakfast, and head to the cottage. I'd toil until nightfall, then return to Shoreside, have dinner, and tuck up into bed.

At first, I was content to listen to the waves cresting on the coastline while working, but then the quiet got to me. I'd stopped by Mitzi's cottage to say hello. Five minutes into our visit, she became spent. As Brenda saw me to the door, she told me it wasn't uncommon for Mitzi to have a spate of difficult days. She encouraged me to come again later in the week.

I was used to being around people, and the neighborhood was like a ghost town in the off-season. Memorial Day would usher droves of part-timers. Until then, I streamed music over my phone for company.

When Ethan Atlas brought his estimate by on Wednesday, it broke the monotony. We exchanged pleasantries, and he explained he was on his way to a jobsite.

"You've made progress, Ms. Landis," Ethan complimented when I showed him around.

"Kitty, please."

"This is an upgrade," he paused, smiling, "Kitty."

I felt a blush stain my cheeks. "I sliced through the carpet pad with a utility knife then rolled it in sections. Once the parlor's cleaned out, I'll move outside and scrape the siding."

"I know you want to be responsible for all the painting, but leave some jobs for us," he teased.

Fee had been after me to invite Ethan for a drink, and I toyed with the idea. There was something about him that drew me, beyond his good looks and friendly personality—a sense of familiarity I shouldn't feel for someone I'd just met. But then I thought, what if he had a girlfriend? What if I wasn't his type? What then? I didn't want things to become awkward.

Ethan pulled a sheaf of papers from under his arm. "Speaking of jobs—I brought a contract for you to sign. There's a copy for your records."

I read through the agreement. Everything was in order. I scrawled my signature on his set of papers, passed them over, then dug in my overall pocket. "Here, I had keys cut for you at Harbor Hardware."

"Did your friend make it home?" Ethan asked as I walked with him to his truck. His face reddened, and it occurred to me—he wasn't interested in me. He was interested in Fee.

"Yes, she's safely back in Santa Beatriz. I'm hoping I can persuade her to fly out again later this summer."

We said our goodbyes. A devilish grin curving my lips, I hurried inside to text Fee. Maybe Ethan could entice her back to Kingfisher Cove.

———

THE LAWNMOWER I ordered online was delivered Friday afternoon. I unboxed it and sat on the kitchen steps beside the dumpster heaped with debris, puzzling over the instruction manual. It was a muggy, overcast day, with the temperature hovering in the high eighties—the type of weather that gave me a headache. I yanked at the neckline of my tank top, feeling overheated and dirty and cranky.

From my peripheral vision, I caught movement. A shiny copper dog settled on its haunches in the driveway, its solemn eyes watchful. My brow furrowing, I got up. The dog wore a collar with a nametag, and I wanted to get a look at the tag. "Where did you come from?"

The dog tolerated my approach, its lean, lithe body vibrating with enthusiasm. I bent, reading the tag but not petting the dog. *Penny*. "The name fits you, doesn't it, girl?"

Penny's rear end shimmied.

Work boots crunched on the clamshell driveway. I rose, my gaze skating up long legs encased in dusty denim, to lean hips and a flat abdomen, to broad shoulders, resting on a pair of eyes a mossy shade of green flecked with hazel.

I knew him.

My pulse quickened, a sort of hyper-awareness floating over me. It couldn't be him, could it? His sun-bleached hair was no longer shaggy—now it was clipped close to his scalp, but I remembered his tattoo.

Pasting on a blank expression, I asked, "Can I help you?"

"I'm looking for Kitty Landis."

"You found her." I roved his face for any signs of recognition, but I couldn't detect any. My skin felt tight. Scorching. Please don't let him notice, I begged.

"Nice to meet you. Thought I'd come by, introduce myself. I'm Jace Atlas, and I'll be in charge of your renovation."

CHAPTER FOURTEEN

I STARED AT JACE'S OUTSTRETCHED HAND, MY BRAIN LAGGING and pulse hammering.

For pity's sake, Kitty, wake up! He doesn't know you. Shake the man's hand before you make it weird.

"Lovely to make your acquaintance, Jace." My voice was even, but when our hands connected, the high voltage current surging up my arm stole my air. Did he feel the same searing charge? His face revealed nothing. I smiled up at him, determined not to allow him to see how affected I was, and nodded to the dog. "Is Penny yours?"

At the mention of her name, Penny woofed, and Jace chuckled. He stooped to scratch her ears. "She's my project manager. It won't be an issue having her here, will it? We're a package deal."

My gaze flew between Penny and Jace. An issue? Months of the Sumans' canines drooling, chewing, and leg humping soured me on dogs. Favoring a root canal without anesthetic rather than put up with them again anytime soon, I scrambled for a reason to refuse. "Is she... er... trained? Housebroken?"

Jace bit his lip as if tickled by my reluctance, regarding me mid ear scratch. A ray of sun escaped from the clouds, illuminating his irises so the hazel flecks glowed like gold. "Miss Penny is as demure and well-mannered as any Southern belle."

His lilting low-country accent curled my toes. *My God, he knows how to switch on the charm.* I was in dangerous territory. "Oh?"

"Yes, ma'am."

I recalled the girl in the bikini with Jace at Shoreside's snack bar. No doubt he had tons of experience with Southern belles. Suddenly fidgety, I stuck my hands in my shorts pockets, eager to end this interaction. To get rid of him. "Uh, I suppose it's okay as long as she doesn't cause any trouble."

"Can I have a look-see at the cottage?" He tossed me a grin as he got to his feet. "It'll give me an idea of what I'm gettin' myself into."

With no graceful way to deny his request, I led Jace inside, feeling exposed in my shorts and tank top. He held the door for Penny, his gaze skimming me before traveling over the dim kitchen.

"Island Power reconnected the electricity yesterday," I babbled to fill the silence, "but with no fixtures, I have to end my workday at dusk. I suppose I could go to Harbor Hardware for some lamps..."

"I'll install temporary fixtures. I'll also bring fans." Jace squatted, examining the holes in the walls where the copper had been harvested. "Ethan clued me in about the pipes—I'm a plumber as well as a licensed general contractor. I'll have it sorted within a week, I'd wager."

"I can't wait to check out of my hotel and camp out here."

"Did Ethan let you know we decided that with the other jobs Atlas has now, I'll be doing most of the work here on my own?"

I observed Penny from the corner of my eye, half-expecting her to lift a leg. Instead, she snuffled innocently along the kitchen baseboards. "No. Won't that delay the project?"

"Nah. A crew will be available when necessary, like for drywalling and laying the floors and such." He pulled his phone from his back pocket, tipping his head toward the doorway connecting the kitchen to the dining room. "You have time for a walk-through with me? I'll make notes."

Being with Jace pushed me off-kilter. Made me nervous, fluttery. But with him in charge of the reno, I figured I might as well get used to his company. In my line of business, I often assumed a poker face. This encounter would be no different. My purse hung from a hook by the pantry. I delved into it, tendering my kitchen sketch and describing the layout changes I wanted.

"Sendler and Grove on the mainland is my go-to for kitchen and bath design. Shall I schedule an appointment for us? Custom cabinetry takes weeks to months to ship."

Picturing us driving together to the mainland, my heart skipped a beat, but I replied, "Absolutely."

"Let me phone them now before they close for the weekend." When Jace completed the call, he told me, "Tuesday at noon. Is it alright if I stop by Monday to measure?"

"But Monday's Memorial Day. Aren't you busy?"

"I'm free in the morning."

"Ethan has the key I had cut." I added, "I'll probably be here, though. I have yardwork."

"He said you're keen to do painting and landscaping yourself."

"R and R isn't in my vocabulary. Plus, the process of transformation is incredibly gratifying." There were rumblings of thunder, and the room darkened. "I was hoping the rain would hold off. Come on, we'll start in the dining room."

Hands braced on his hips in the middle of the room, Jace turned in a circle. "Window, lighting, drywall, flooring, paint."

"I'd like to replace the swinging door going into the kitchen, too."

"You got it."

At the entrance to the parlor, he leaned against the wall, muttering as he typed, "Lighting, drywall, flooring, paint."

"And the built-ins."

"I can fix those up for you." He peeked in the hall bath as we passed it. "Toilet, tile, tub, lighting, medicine cabinet."

In the primary bedroom, I lingered at the French doors. The sea was choppy and the sky an ominous shade. "Did you hear about the mess the squatters left in here?"

"Yeah. I never would've believed it based on how the place is now." Stepping into the en suite, he said, "Nice size. Big enough that you can add a shower."

Gloomy light filtered through the rectangular window above the clawfoot tub. White hexagon subway tile with dark grout stretched across the floor. There was a stained toilet and a pedestal sink with antiquated taps. I'd stacked painting supplies in the corner.

"I don't think a shower is necessary when there's one in the hallway bath."

"No holes in the walls here," Jace noted.

"Only because there was junk three feet deep. It took a whole day to shovel it out."

He scratched his chin. "Unless I hit a snag with the plumbing and it takes longer than anticipated, we can skip ordering the portable potty. We can manage for a week."

"I wish I had running water the other day when I washed the walls—I had to buy gallon jugs of it and use rags and a bucket. Anyhow, now that the walls are prepped, I plan to paint in here this weekend. That is, if the storm tempers the humidity." I caught a whiff of Jace's soapy-scented cologne. My knees weakened. I needed to get outside where I could breathe. I edged toward the bathroom door. "I'll show you the paver patio before the downpour."

We stepped outside. Gulping, I pretended not to study Jace as a bead of perspiration trickled between my cleavage. I was hot and bothered by him, and nothing about his demeanor hinted he was similarly afflicted. That scarcely seemed fair.

We discussed sourcing pavers to replace the crumbling ones. Wicked storm clouds massed over the sea, the wind whipping. I put a hand to my hair. The atmosphere shifted, a tang of ozone permeating the air. Lightning flashed, then a crack of thunder shook the ground. "Whoa."

Jace sighed, his gaze on the violent horizon. Voice husky, he murmured, "I love storms, especially savage storms. I'm always struck by how we're at nature's mercy. We see ourselves as significant, yet we're really inconsequential. Eh, I'm getting philosophic."

I understood what he meant. How many times had I fled to the shore as a teen, my face to the moon, inhaling the salty brine and philosophizing? I'd been a waif of a girl, small but vitally alive. Pining for something I couldn't verbalize and feeling like a tiny grain of sand amongst billions. Shutting my eyes, I confessed, "It's my little corner of the world."

When I opened them again, I discovered Jace focused on me. Our gazes met and held. We connected. It was as if he could see into my soul.

A raindrop splashed on my cheek, and I cleared my throat, glancing away. The spell broke.

"I suppose I'd best be going. Penny!" She was down by the water, her snout in a clump of sea oats. Jace brought his fingers to his mouth and whistled. Penny trotted through the sand up the gentle slope of the yard to her master's side as the rain gathered force.

After bolting the door behind Jace and Penny, I went to pack my stuff to return to Shoreside, wondering why I felt so unsettled.

CHAPTER FIFTEEN

I was surprised to see Jace had already installed the overhead fixtures he'd mentioned when I showed up at the cottage mid-morning Saturday. In addition, there were box fans lined up against the kitchen wall. Warmth spread across my chest at his thoughtfulness, but I reminded myself he was merely doing his job.

Pushing window sashes up, I wedged the fans inside the frames to circulate the air. Although there was a furnace for chilly nights, my grandparents hadn't installed central air conditioning—being near the sea usually made for comfortable summer temps.

I painted ceilings before beginning the en suite bathroom, working late into the night Saturday. Thanks to the overhead fixtures Jace mounted, I had ample light. On Sunday, I primed the bathroom walls, then once they were dry, rolled on a layer of blue paint called Peacock. After the second coat, I stood back, inspecting the walls for missed spots but not locating any. The color was beautiful. Calming. I adored the results.

I crossed my fingers that a pumice stone would save the toilet, tub, and pedestal sink. Once Jace overhauled the plumbing, I planned to scrub the tile floors, too. Yawning, I packed up my painting supplies and went out the French doors for a breather before mowing the lawn.

Children's voices drifted to the patio. I put my hand to my temple like a visor. There they were. A pair of kids were setting up a badminton net in a backyard a few cottages away. Early birds. The island would soon be flooded with vacationers.

I downed a bottle of water then rolled my neck to ease the kinks. Days of physical exertion were taking their toll. My body ached, and I felt like a wreck—sweat ringed my tank top, and I had paint in my hair.

Screw it. I'd knock off early and pass the remainder of the afternoon lounging beside Shoreside's pool.

───

MONDAY, I negotiated around vehicles clogging Sand Dollar Way. At the beachfront homes flanking Randcliffe Cottage, families settled in for the season. Parking was at a premium, and it would be that way the entire summer. With the dumpster occupying my driveway, I had to park at the end of the street and hoof it to the cottage.

I'd finished mowing the front lawn when a charcoal gray crew cab truck double-parked at the curb. I caught sight of Penny in the passenger seat, then Jace stepped down from behind the wheel. His hair was slicked back from a recent shower, and he wore faded jeans and a black tee.

I raised a hand in greeting, self-conscious of my appearance. Switching the mower off, I pushed it until it was against the cottage, exchanging it for my rake.

"Hard at work, I see," Jace teased. He had a measuring tape in one hand, a notebook under his arm.

I returned his smile—how could I not? "The door's unlocked. Help yourself."

I raked a section of the yard while Jace measured.

Depositing an armful of grass clippings in a lawn and leaf bag, I grabbed my rake and pivoted, jumping when I noticed him a few feet away.

"Didn't intend to scare you," he said with a chuckle. "I got my measurements. My compliments on the painting. I'm amazed at the progress you've made."

Why did I feel as shy as a schoolgirl? "I never would've been able to get it done this weekend if you hadn't put up the fixtures."

"No problem. I swung by early Saturday to install them in case you decided to work into the wee hours."

"Well, I appreciate it."

Jace drawled, "I aim to please, Ms. Landis."

My cheeks flamed. "Call me Kitty. Everyone does."

"Alright." His gaze appraised the yard. "This how you're gonna celebrate the holiday, Kitty? Toiling in the blazing sun instead of barbecuing?"

"I don't know anyone to barbecue with," I replied mildly, ignoring the zing of realization that Jace was building up to something.

"You know me." He arched an eyebrow. "And Ethan. Y'all come over to ours for the afternoon."

"I-I couldn't," I protested. My hair was wet with perspiration and strewn with grass. The mower had kicked up dust, a fine film of it covering my skin. I didn't have anything suitable to wear. There were a million reasons, not least of all that I was tongue-tied in Jace's presence. "I wouldn't want to impose. Really."

"No imposition. We host an open house every Memorial Day. Neighbors filter in and out to eat brisket, drink beer, and kick off the summer." Flipping his notebook to a clean page, he wrote on it then tore off the sheet. "Our address. I insist. You're gonna burn yourself out if you don't take a break, Kitty."

He had a point. Instead of protesting further, I accepted the paper, my pulse ratcheting when our fingers brushed.

"Shindig's at three."

I argued with myself while locking up the house and walking to my car. Despite the way being around Jace twisted me inside out, I *did* deserve a break. And brisket? My mouth watered. For frugality's sake, I no longer ordered room service at Shoreside. Instead, I'd gone to the grocery store for fruit and granola bars. My mini-fridge in my room was stocked with sandwich fixin's for lunch and bagged salad for dinner. The notion of real food—hot, homemade food—was enticing.

The clerk's attitude at Shoreside's dress shop was decidedly judgmental when I crossed the threshold. I'd washed my hands and face in the lobby restroom, but there was no denying I was a disaster. Her face pinched, she inquired, "May I assist you, madam?"

I demurred, thumbing through the racks of fashionable sundresses. Fee was right—the shop had divine clothes. Throwing caution to the wind, I selected three dresses, two pairs of sandals, and a wicker handbag. When the salesclerk rang them up, the total had me pining for smelling salts. Figuring I'd try the clothes on later and return what I didn't care for, I charged them to my room.

Before heading upstairs, I inquired at the front desk about a pie from The Seafarer. Manners wouldn't permit me to attend a gathering empty-handed. The manager was accommodating. "Certainly, Ms. Landis. We'll have our signature lemon meringue pie here for you by three."

While showering, my excitement about attending the barbecue blossomed. It had been too long since I'd socialized, and I was curious about Jace's family. Jace. I itched to know more about him.

I dried my hair, my mind on our moment the other day before the storm. I'd felt a connection. He must've, too.

Perhaps I was a fool. He hadn't given me any indication he was interested in me beyond contractor and client, but part of me wanted to impress Jace. He'd only seen me at my worst—dripping with sweat and clad in filthy clothes. What would he think of me in an expensive dress with my hair loose on my shoulders?

My cell rang from where I'd tossed it on the bed. Putting my comb on the bureau, I glimpsed at the screen. Fee. I typically shared everything with her, but my impulse was to keep mum about the barbecue. I had sworn to my bestie that romance wasn't on my radar, after all.

I didn't answer, letting the call go to voicemail.

CHAPTER SIXTEEN

I DECIDED ON AN UNDERSTATED COBALT-AND-WHITE STRIPED dress with a woven straw belt and espadrilles. After curling the ends of my hair, I applied light makeup. Then I arranged an Uber, picking up the pie from the front desk before waiting for my ride by the resort's grand entrance.

Jace lived in Upper King, the working class northern portion of the island. Homes there were crammed together even closer than the ones in Lower King, and finding parking was a nuisance. The driver idled at the curb of a two-story tan bungalow with patriotic bunting spanning the porch railings. An Atlas All Trades van was parked in the driveway behind what I recognized as Jace's Ram crew cab.

Shifting my wicker handbag and balancing the bakery box containing the pie, I alighted from the Uber. At neighboring homes, people gathered, conversing and laughing and eating. My mouth salivated at the smell of grilled meat. As I made my way up the sidewalk, a group of barefoot kids playing tag clipped me. I scrabbled to hold onto the bakery box.

There was the screech of a screen door, then Ethan emerged from beneath the covered porch. He hustled down the stairs, scolding the kids with, "Watch it, you guys!"

"I'm okay," I assured him as he took the bakery box from me. Now that I knew he and Jace were brothers, their likeness was apparent—the straight nose, square jaw, and boyish smile. No wonder he'd seemed familiar.

"Glad you could make it, Kitty. The party's in the backyard. Come through the house."

Ethan escorted me across the porch to the front door, which opened on a modest but comfortably furnished living room decorated in earth tones. Classic rock pumped from stereo speakers, hindering conversation. I trailed him into a cheerful yellow kitchen beyond the living room where the back door was located.

"My brother Chris is the pitmaster of the family," Ethan confided, projecting his voice. "Brisket's fresh out of the smoker. Did you bring your appetite?"

"I'm starving," I promised.

"You've lost weight."

I'd noticed my clothes were looser. "Must be all the manual labor I've been doing."

We stepped outside onto a deck. The backyard was a neat, well-tended square of lawn bordered by flowering bushes and hostas. A dozen people were seated at wood picnic tables, Jace among them. He got up to meet us, his eyes glowing as his gaze scanned me. "Kitty."

"Jace."

"Everyone," he announced, "this is Kitty Landis. She bought Randcliffe Cottage, and Atlas is revamping it."

The attendees called out hellos, their expressions inquisitive. I waved in response, my face prickling with a blush. Penny scampered up to me as if we were old pals and pushed her muzzle into my leg. Leaning down, I patted her silky head.

A man resembling Jace and Ethan stood at a folding table carving a hunk of steaming meat on a platter. He must be Chris. He said over his shoulder, "Perfect timing, Kitty.

Almost time to eat. I'm waiting on the wings. Jace, grab her a drink, will ya?"

Ethan placed the pie on a banquet table laden with dishes. I was relieved I'd had the foresight to buy it. A red cooler was at the base of the steps. Jace opened it, asking, "Beer, bottled water, or soda?"

"Water, please."

Jace dried the bottle with the hem of his shirt before passing it to me. I gave him a grateful smile and screwed off the lid.

"Kitty?"

I turned.

It was a blonde woman in her sixties with Jace's green eyes. "I'm Jace's mom, Elaine. Welcome, honey."

I thanked her for her hospitality, and she directed me to an unoccupied picnic table. Ten minutes of polite conversation later, I'd learned Elaine had been born on the island and was now a widow whose husband passed two autumns previous. A mother to six kids and a grandmother to three, she had retired from her cashier job at Jensen's Market in March.

"Jackson's my eldest," she said, indicating a man at another table holding a tow-headed girl on his knee. "He's a fisherman. He and his wife Andrea have twins—Maliyah and Larissa. Then there's Ethan and Jace and Chris. They operate Atlas All Trades. Chris is married to Steph. Candy's my only girl. She does the accounting for the business in the evenings. Normally she'd be here, but her newborn has a cold, and she and her husband thought they ought to skip this year's cookout. My baby's Joey. He works on Jackson's trawler. He's around somewhere."

Penny at his heels, Jace settled beside me with a plate of potato salad and chicken wings.

"My stars," Elaine gasped. "I forgot to bring the macaroni salad and deviled eggs from the fridge."

Jace grinned amiably at me when she rushed inside. "Ma will gab your ear off if you aren't careful."

"I feel like I've known her forever."

"That's what everyone says."

"There are so many names to remember," I said. "What's it like to have such a large family?"

"Chaotic."

I asked, "Never a dull moment, I presume?"

"You presume correct. The stories I could tell—"

"Kitty," Elaine beckoned from the buffet line, gesturing for me to join her.

I took the paper plate Elaine presented me, choosing a thick slice of brisket and a generous serving of macaroni salad along with plasticware and a napkin. Once back at our seats, we tucked into our food.

Elaine scooped a spoonful of baked beans, leveling her green gaze on me. "I tend to monopolize conversations, I'm afraid. Too many years of chitchat with customers at the grocery store—it's a tough habit to break. I want to know about *you*. Ethan says you're a realtor?"

I nodded. "I co-own a brokerage in California with a friend."

"My word, how did you come to buy here when California is chock full of coastal property? You aren't from the island, are you?"

Tipping my water bottle for a lengthy swig to delay answering, I grappled to formulate a reply. If I divulged too many details, Jace might connect the dots and realize Kitty Landis was in fact Katrina Randcliffe. That would be... uncomfortable. I side-eyed him, finding his attention pinpointed on me. Swallowing, I wiped my mouth with a napkin. "I grew up in Boston, but my family and I vacationed on Kingfisher Cove. When the cottage came up for auction, I jumped on it."

"Oh, yes. Those beach homes aren't often put on the

market," Elaine said. "Some of them have been in families for generations. Aren't you lucky!"

Discussion veered to the renovation. Jace brought up our design appointment at Sendler and Grove tomorrow.

Elaine said, "It's putting the cart before the horse, but there's an antique shop on the mainland you should visit. It's huge. Three floors."

"I'll check it out," I replied. "There's not a stick of furniture in the cottage."

The child who'd been on Jackson's lap earlier approached Elaine, and Elaine put her arm around the girl's waist. "This is Larissa, one of Jackson's daughters."

"Grandma, can we have cake now?"

"You bet, pumpkin." Elaine unfolded from the picnic table bench. "Let's cut you a slice."

An auburn-haired woman around my age slid into Elaine's vacant seat.

Jace introduced us. "Kitty, this is my sister-in-law Steph. Chris's wife."

I asked, "Chris, the pitmaster?"

Steph laughed. "The one and only."

"That brisket rivaled any I've tasted," I said.

"It's why I married him." Steph winked. "I just had to come over and meet the woman who outbid Jace."

What? My forehead wrinkled in confusion, I regarded Jace. "You bid on the cottage during the auction?"

"I tried," he said, unconcerned. He shrugged. "You win some, you lose some."

The weight of Jace's eyes was heavy on me. I made small talk with Steph, putting on a show that I wasn't dismayed by her revelation. While unsure how I felt about it, my guts were in knots.

Wasn't it a conflict of interest for Atlas to take on the reno if their general contractor lost a bidding war for said property? I'd placed an enormous amount of trust in the company.

What if Jace had an ax to grind? Was my trust misplaced? And, if the whole thing was no big deal, why not disclose he'd been a bidder when we first met at the cottage?

When there was a lull in the conversation, I nonchalantly inquired where the bathroom was.

"There's one in the kitchen and another at the top of the stairs," Steph said.

"I'll be back," I replied as I stood, studiously avoiding Jace's eyes, and went to throw my plate into a trashcan by the deck.

Elaine and her twin granddaughters advanced on me, slices of cake in hand. Elaine urged, "Help yourself to dessert, Kitty."

I told them I was headed to the restroom and hastened up the stairs, craving a minute to collect my thoughts. The bathroom off the kitchen was engaged, so I walked through the living room to the stairway leading to the upper level. Family photos on the wall drew my eye. There were school portraits of Jace and his siblings. My lips parted when I saw an informal snap of the Atlas family taken at the beach.

The pretty girl in the bikini I'd seen with Jace at Shoreside was there, front and center. She was evidently his sister Candy.

CHAPTER SEVENTEEN

I'D STAYED AT THE COOKOUT ANOTHER HOUR VISITING WITH THE
Atlas family. I liked them—they were friendly and welcoming
—however, I longed for solitude.

Begging off with the excuse I was tired and declining
Jace's offer to drive me to my hotel, I scheduled an Uber from
my cell. I didn't want to be alone with him until I gathered
my thoughts.

Sleep was impossible that night. My brain refused to
quiet.

Upon seeing Jace and the girl at Shoreside, I'd leaped to
conclusions. What if, instead of tucking tail and scurrying to
the cottage in defeat, I strode with confidence to that snack
bar and greeted Jace? After he introduced Candy, I'd have
explained my quandary, and we would've swapped email
addresses. Kept in contact. Our chemistry was undeniable—a
relationship had been in the cards for us. Shoot, in an alternate life, we might have ended up married.

Abandoning my bed, I sat on the lounger on the balcony
outside my room and took in the roar of the surf breaking
against the shore. The night was crisp and tranquil, the sky
dotted with stars reflecting on the water.

I tended to be hard on myself. I was far too judgmental of eighteen-year-old Katrina. Although mature beyond her age in many ways, she had been woefully naïve in others. So she made an assumption. Her world had been rocked. She hadn't been thinking straight and coped to the best of her abilities.

Allow her, and yourself, a measure of grace.

Jace asked at the lighthouse whether I believed in fate. During the intervening years, I rarely wallowed in what could've been. I was too pragmatic for that—it was a waste of energy. Truthfully, in my heart of hearts, I did feel robbed. Was fate attempting to right a wrong by granting us another chance?

Well, it didn't matter. Before Labor Day, I was flying home to Santa Beatriz.

What about a fling?

I rolled my eyes and grimaced. Thirty-three-year-old Kitty was also leaping to conclusions, wasn't she? A level-headed woman wouldn't drive herself batty over-thinking. Jace was a cordial guy. I was by myself on a holiday, and he'd invited me to his family's home. End of story. It didn't translate to him wanting to slam me against a wall and make mad, passionate love.

Without a doubt, the topic of Jace bidding on Randcliffe Cottage must be broached. What was his story? My gut told me he didn't have nefarious intentions, but I'd bring the subject up tomorrow. I'd also test the waters and flirt, to gauge his feelings. That wouldn't hurt anything, would it?

Pacified by my plan, I crawled into bed and slept.

JACE WAS at the cottage when I arrived at eleven, Penny nowhere to be found.

"Hey. I ordered patio pavers from Advantage Brickworks. They'll be delivered later this month," he said, not glancing up from his tablet when I climbed into the cushy leather passenger seat of his Ram and fastened my seatbelt.

"Hey yourself." The interior was imbued with his soapy cologne. My body responded to the fragrance with a visceral tug.

"I held off placing the flooring order because I wanted to confirm you're certain about the hardwood."

"I am. But I prefer tile in the hallway bathroom," I answered, lowering my sunglasses to consider him over the frames. Today he was dressed "business casual" in a formfitting button-up and khakis that showcased his tight physique. He hadn't shaved, his scruff giving him an edgy look. No question about it—Jace Atlas was a stud.

"We'll acquire tile through Sendler and Grove." Glancing from his tablet, his eyes widened as his gaze swept me. I'd selected one of my new outfits from Shoreside's shop, a floaty coral maxi dress I knew suited my fair complexion. Jace's rapt exploration paused at my décolletage, and his face suffused with color. Coughing, he refocused on his tablet. "That fancy getup'll be wasted on errands. Can I treat you to a meal once our business is concluded?"

So Jace wasn't immune to my allure. I smirked in satisfaction, my rejoinder flirtatious. "You can, on the condition *I* pick the restaurant."

"Your wish is my command," he said smoothly. "Allow me to put this flooring order through, and we'll hit the road— I need an estimated delivery date. It'd throw a wrench in the works if the appliances are shipped prior to the floor installation. You got an idea what you'd like?"

While Jace finalized the order, I unlocked my phone and searched my bookmarked web pages. "There's a retro line I'm contemplating. I emailed the company to ask about shipping times, and they responded there's an eight-week lead time."

"Done." Jace snapped the cover on his tablet shut.

I passed him my cell. "They're pricey but cool."

The line included refrigerators, ranges, microwaves, dishwashers, and small appliances with a 1950s flair. The models were available in a half-dozen pastels. "Extremely cool vibe," Jace agreed. "Which color?"

"I'm torn between the blue and the green."

A car horn honked. We were double-parked on Sand Dollar Way in front of the cottage, blocking a vintage Bentley's passage. Brenda was driving. Mitzi sat in the passenger seat, wearing oversize Jackie O sunglasses and a wide-brimmed purple hat. Jace returned my phone, and I waved to my neighbors as he switched on the ignition. He maneuvered past the beachfront properties and merged onto Starfish Avenue.

An old Eagles ballad was on the radio. Jace adjusted the volume lower. "Kitty, yesterday…"

I looked at him with expectation.

"I wanna clear the air." He glimpsed at me briefly before reverting his gaze to the road. "When Steph told you about me bidding on the cottage? It upset you, didn't it?"

"It startled me." I clasped my hands in my lap but maintained a light tone. "I was going to grill you about it today."

"I didn't mention bidding on Randcliffe Cottage because it's irrelevant. I'm a believer in things happening for a reason, and I want you to know, I'm not bitter about losing it, Kitty."

Jace sounded sincere, but that wasn't enough. I needed to uncover his motive behind the bidding. "Are you in the market for a house?"

"I live with Ma—so does Joey—if that's what you're asking, and I've been saving money for ages for my own place. You know how expensive homes are on the island, even in Upper King. When I learned about the auction, I'd been facing a dilemma, and I told myself to let the universe steer me."

"What dilemma?" Was I prying? Possibly. "Sorry, I shouldn't have asked. It's none of my affair."

"No, no. It's alright," he said. "I've gotten into carpentry and furniture making, and I've been kicking around parting ways with Atlas All Trades."

"What does your family think about that?"

Jace pulled a face. "That's just it. As far as they're concerned, woodworking is a hobby. They aren't aware that a friend of mine on the mainland owns a woodshop, and he's asked me to be partners. When I was outbid, it was as if the universe determined I should buy into the partnership rather than buy a home."

"But you're hesitant, so you're not totally sold on it," I conjectured.

"No, I'm not." He lifted a shoulder as he deftly piloted the truck onto the parkway bridge. "All Trades is my birthright, and I never questioned abandoning it 'til recently. The obligation can be... it... smothers me sometimes, but I hate disappointing my family."

I struggled to find proper words. I was in a unique position, a position where I empathized with Jace's predicament. Katrina Randcliffe was smothered by her birthright, too. Her future had been meticulously plotted and planned. It stretched in front of her. Suffocated her. Endless duty and obligation—her legacy as a Randcliffe descendant. Jace was me fifteen years ago. The difference was that his family wasn't as uncompromising as Grandmother. "I can't imagine the people I met yesterday wanting to force you to stay. They wouldn't want you to be miserable."

Jace rubbed the back of his neck. "It's risky, striking out on your own."

Tell me about it. "It's even more so when you don't have a support system," I pointed out, "and that's something you've got that many people don't. I mean, I didn't."

"It must've been terrifying being alone," Jace replied huskily.

"I wasn't entirely alone—I had my bestie Fee at my side.

We shared a dream and pooled our resources to form our brokerage. The first years were lean. We ate ramen for every meal."

He extended a hand to squeeze mine, his touch eliciting goosebumps. "I admire your chutzpah."

"Shucks, you're making me blush, Jace," I said in jest, but I cracked my window, seeking oxygen. "In all seriousness, you should take the plunge. I'd be happy to commission a table for the dining room."

Yielding to a red light, he faced me, awarding me with a lopsided grin that caused my stomach to cartwheel. "Sketch it out, and I'll see what I can do."

CHAPTER EIGHTEEN

Sendler and Grove was a thirty-minute jaunt from the Cove, located in an upscale area. The stucco building was the size of a football field, surrounded by lush landscaping and palmetto trees. We were received in the lobby by a woman in her forties wearing an elegant fuchsia pantsuit. Jace said, "Kitty, this is Louella Benn, kitchen and bath artiste."

Louella laughed, and we shook hands. "Jace flatters me." She ushered us through the showroom and up to her over-sized desk in the mezzanine, imploring us to sit then fetching refreshments. Once we were served ice-cold sparkling water, she slid into her swivel chair. "I used the dimensions Jace emailed to prepare mockups of your kitchen and bath spaces, but describe your vision."

I pulled my phone from my purse. "Here's my kitchen Pinterest board. The floor will be a medium brown hardwood, and the walls will be white shiplap. I want cabinets like these and a white porcelain farmhouse sink with a sprayer like this one."

"If only all my clients were as prepared as you, Kitty!" She spun her chair to a bookshelf and grabbed a catalogue, flipping it open for my perusal. "These cabinets are comparable to your inspiration pics."

"Yes. I like the shaker style in Alpine Snow, with the glass cabinets option on either side of the sink, and the quartz countertop in Abalone Shell."

Louella jotted part numbers on a notepad. "What about your backsplash?"

"It depends on which appliances I choose. Let me show you what I was thinking." I brought up the website I'd shared with Jace and gave the phone to Louella so she could scroll. "I figure either Jadeite Green or Robin's Egg Blue will look fabulous, but I'm leaning toward the blue."

"Those appliances are exceptional. Clever of you to create a neutral backdrop to flaunt them." Her finger tapping her cheek, Louella asked, "What color cookery do you have?"

"I don't. I'll get new dishes and pots and pans, but I'd prefer the backsplash to coordinate with the appliances."

"No Pyrex or Fiestaware you want displayed?"

I shook my head. "I'll curate a glassware collection based on the kitchen design."

"Hold on a sec," Louella said, standing. She handed me my phone then disappeared between display racks. Returning minutes later with an armful of tile sample boards, she placed two of them on the desktop in front of me. One board was tiled in shades of blue, the other in shades of green. "As you can see, there are swatches identical to the appliances. You can go with either a single color backsplash or mix a customized one."

"A customized palette, definitely," I said. "With white grout."

"Here." Louella plucked a jade tile from the board and placed it on the desk. "They're removable, so you can experiment with combinations. I'd refine down to six colors max."

I steepled my fingers, cognizant of Jace's indulgent chuckle. He teased, "You're in your element, aren't you?"

"I have to admit, this is fun."

"While you do that, I'll prep bathroom options," Louella said.

Settling on the robin's egg appliances, I picked the shade of tile that paired with it, along with five other harmonizing hues of blue and green similar to sea glass I'd gathered from the beach as a child. "I plan to decorate the cottage in these colors, so they're perfect for the backsplash."

Louella took note of my choices then replaced the tiled boards with two others, rectangular and hexagonal tiles in a multitude of colors. "Now, the bathroom."

"This is what I was thinking for the shower surround and halfway up the bathroom walls." I indicated the rectangular tile in white. "Then these white hexagons for the floor. Dark grout for both, like the en suite bath has."

"May I suggest," Louella passed me a catalogue of plumbing fixtures, "the Remington or Clubhouse suite."

I studied the images. The Remington spoke to me, reminding me of the period fixtures in the en suite bathroom. I opted for a console sink with chrome legs, a tub and toilet from the same line, chrome faucets with porcelain accents, and glass shower doors.

"To summarize the kitchen," Louella said. "Alpine Snow shaker cabinetry and Abalone Shell quartz counters. Glass cabinets flanking the farmhouse sink. Chrome faucet with pullout spray. Customized tile backsplash with white grout. In the bathroom we have rectangle subway tiles in a quantity for a half wall and to surround the bathtub. Hexagon tiled floor. Slate grout. Remington suite with chrome option fixtures."

She plugged all of my selections into the design program on her laptop, rendering a 3-D image of the kitchen, then generating one for the bathroom. She printed copies for Jace and me.

We scrutinized our printouts. Jace said, "Appears all the bases are covered."

"They're exactly like my vision boards." I told Louella, "Let's do it."

While she calculated what was owed, I took my wallet from my wicker handbag.

"Since Jace is responsible for the installation, your total includes materials and my consultation fee," she said, then gave me the figure.

"Oof." Blanching, I presented my card.

"Shipping's on average four to six weeks, but I'll keep Jace updated." Louella placed our paperwork in a folder with the Sendler and Grove insignia and sent us on our way.

Exiting through the main doors to the parking lot, Jace put his arm around me. "Let's have lunch. We'll fix you up with a stiff drink to help you recover from the sticker shock."

Chewing an olive, I guzzled my dirty martini. "I thought I'd pass out when Louella told me the total."

Jace sat across from me in a booth at a local restaurant. "You went pale."

"If I'd had on pearls, I would've clutched them," I confided. "I'm not accustomed to spending thousands at the drop of a hat. Fee jokes about my tightfisted habits."

"Here I pictured you living a high-flying California lifestyle."

"I'm *not* a high-flyer," I replied dryly. "I live in a drab shoebox and drive a seven-year-old car."

Jace cocked his head. "I gathered your brokerage was successful."

"Oh, it is. I credit my frugality for its success. It took a lot of sacrifice."

The waitress appeared. I requested a vat of fettucine

Alfredo, and Jace chose a ribeye and a baked potato. When she left to put in our order, he rested his elbows on the table. "What do you do in your spare time?"

I snorted. "What spare time? This is the first vacation I've taken in years."

"Some vacation. You've been working your fingers to the bone," he tsked.

I drained my martini, feeling tipsy. "Not the last couple days, I haven't. Back to the grind tomorrow. Did I tell you I have an impending garden shed delivery?"

"No, you didn't. Do you need me to put it together?"

I shook my head. Maybe the martini on an empty stomach wasn't the smartest decision. I grabbed a breadstick from the basket and nibbled at it. "The plumbing takes precedence. Once I have the shed together, my focus will be scraping the siding."

"Painting the cottage is a massive undertaking, Kitty," Jace warned. "You don't want me to assign it to my guys?"

"I told Ethan I'd paint, ergo it is not included in the bid. At least I have all summer."

We discussed plumbing and drywalling until the waitress came to our table with our entrées. Jace cut his steak, narrowing his gaze on me. "You can't travel to the island and not carve out time for leisure. I'm going to make it my personal mission to see that you do."

CHAPTER NINETEEN

Fee's voice sounded tinny over my cellphone speaker. "That's nice that you met your neighbor and all... but why didn't you tell me before that your general contractor is the Jace from your past?"

After lunch, Jace dropped me at the cottage, and instead of changing into my mowing clothes and weeding flower beds as I'd intended, I drove to Shoreside. The carb-laden lunch made me drowsy. Vegging on my balcony lounger, I'd dialed Fee, filling her in on the latest. "This is our first time talking since he made his appearance."

"And you're telling me he didn't recognize you? Shut uuup. It's not as if you've changed *that* much."

"That's debatable. In any case, he didn't say anything, and neither did I." I paused and yawned. "Of course I ID'd him right away—I have a memory for faces—but I was caught off guard. I didn't have to play dumb, I was struck dumb."

"There was a mob of bidders at the auction. None of them stood out to me," Fee said, adding with a hint of speculation, "but that's quite the coincidence. I didn't realize general contractors could afford beach houses of that caliber. Atlas All Trades must make bank."

My bestie's skepticism registered through the phone line. "My initial reaction mirrors yours, but Jace's explanation today was plausible," I replied, turning self-deprecating. "The island's not huge. I should've predicted I'd encounter people from back in the day."

"Kitty, Kitty, Kitty," Fee sing-songed. "You've gotten yourself embroiled. What am I gonna do with you?"

I put my head in my hands, repentant. "I know."

"Will you tell him?"

"I'm not sure. Too much time has passed now. I should've bit the bullet that day."

"What's he like?"

"Attractive. Built. Magnetic personality that oozes Southern charm."

Laughing, Fee said, "A triple threat."

Before she could propose I hop into bed with Jace, I switched the subject to the cottage. "What can I do to cajole you into booking a flight to come paint with me?"

"Haha! I have a valid excuse—I landed a new listing today. I'm tied up for the foreseeable."

Ugh. "I guess I'm on my own."

OVER THE SUBSEQUENT DAYS, Jace and I established a routine. To allay complaints from my neighbors, our workday commenced at 9 a.m. We concentrated on our individual duties then shared lunch while sitting on the patio. When Jace headed home at five, I'd walk over to Mitzi's cottage, checking to see if she was up for a visit. If she was, we'd chat while drinking a Mauve Madness. Occasionally, we shared an evening meal.

Penny acting as my supervisor, I stuck with outdoor projects while Jace saw to the plumbing repairs. Once I'd constructed my garden shed, I was consumed with the tedious task of scraping the siding. More than once I questioned my sanity for assigning it to myself, eventually caving and running to Harbor Hardware for a hand sander. Even with the sander, it was slow going.

Within a week and a half, Jace had the water restored and a new water heater fitted. I was thrilled to have a functioning bathroom and was strategizing relocating to the cottage when the hardwood flooring was delivered.

"It'll take a few days to acclimate the wood. Then I have to lay it, sand it, stain it, and apply poly. Best to hold off 'til it's finished, I'm afraid," Jace told me.

I groaned. My room at the resort was burning a hole in my pocket, along with the car rental fees. I was seriously considering buying a secondhand car, so I could turn in the rental. "How long do you think that'll be?"

Jace used a utility knife to slice through the tape on the boxes. "Week or so. These boards need to be spaced and cross-stacked for air circulation. I'll schedule the crew to drywall while they're acclimating."

"I was under the impression it would take all summer to get the cottage renovated." I kneeled to gather boards, stacking them as Jace instructed. "At this rate, we'll be finished by the Fourth of July."

"It's all by design. There are built-ins to build, trim to install, windows to repair, and on and on and on." Jace's eyes crinkled, a sign he was amused. "I also heard rumors about window boxes and a pergola?"

My face heated. I felt sheepish. "Am I getting ahead of myself?"

"Just a tad." Jace mopped the sweat from his brow, winking at me. "Trust the process."

We threw the boxes in the dumpster. When we shut the door, Penny was sitting in the kitchen holding her empty plastic water dish in her mouth, a question in her caramel eyes.

I bent, skimming a hand over Penny's glossy coat. "Someone's thirsty."

Jace took the dish, filling it from a chilled bottle of water from his cooler. "Here, Pen."

"Being project manager sure is exhausting," I quipped while Penny daintily lapped at her bowl. She wasn't anything like the Sumans' undisciplined mutts—she was a lady. I was under the misapprehension I wasn't a dog person, but she'd won me over.

Jace unearthed cans of soda for us from the partially melted ice in the cooler, passing me a diet cola. "Wanna sit outside?"

"Let's knock off for the day and walk along the shore."

"You and Penny start without me. Once I change into the shorts I have in my bag, I'll be down."

In the parlor, I unlaced my sneakers and stepped from them then peeled off my socks. I whistled for Penny, and she hurtled past me out the French doors and across the lawn into the surf. As I trailed her, I popped the top on my soda and drank thirstily. The sand was powdery and sizzled from the afternoon sun, burning my soles. Penny barked, zooming around me in circles, challenging me to frolic with her.

Setting my soda in the sand, I entered the water, halting when I was knee deep. It was blessedly cool. Heavenly. I closed my eyes and put my face to the sky. A wave broke against my thighs, wetting the hem of my cutoffs.

"We should bring our bathing suits and leave them at the cottage."

I opened my eyes and turned around. Jace was in shorts and nothing else. And I'd thought he was sexy while clothed…

Penny found a twig. Jace tossed it for her, then she sped to fetch it. I waded in deeper, not caring my tank and shorts were drenched.

The waves swirled around Jace's corded legs. "I forgot to mention that Ma was asking after you."

"Was she?"

"The whole clan comes to the house Sundays for supper, and she requested I invite you."

"She's kind," I murmured. Was it wise to become a fixture at Atlas family dinners? I'd known Jace for a short time, but he and Penny were already becoming part of the fabric of my life. It disturbed me that after we said our goodbyes in the evenings, I noticed their absence. Rolling my shoulder, I winced. "Oof, I'm sore. And I probably have another week of sanding before the siding is ready for primer."

"Allow me." Jace closed the distance between us, motioning I should face away from him. When I did, he placed his hands on my shoulder blades, applying gentle pressure with his thumbs.

I gasped, knowing I was playing with fire but submitting to his touch regardless. Dropping my chin on my chest, I reveled in the feel of Jace's calloused hands on my exposed flesh. He kneaded the length of my trapezius muscles with the pads of his fingers, easing the tension held there.

He put his lips to the shell of my ear. "Please come to dinner, Kitty."

I would've agreed to anything in that moment.

CHAPTER TWENTY

Assigned to provide dessert for Sunday supper, I had my Uber driver stop at the gelateria on Cleary Beach's boardwalk before driving me to the Atlas residence. Lingering in the backyard after our meal of grilled burgers and corn on the cob, I dished servings of gelato.

"Can I give her a taste?" I asked Jace, nodding to Penny. Observing the sweet vizsla play with Jackson and Andrea's twins, I'd been witness to her impeccable behavior. Maliyah and Larissa were rambunctious, wrestling and rolling around, but Penny was the epitome of mellow. She deserved a treat. "It's vanilla."

"Sure," he said as he collected plates.

Penny sat immobile as a statue, licking her chops. Her eyes chased my movements, but she didn't budge. I praised her, putting the bowl on the grass, and she went to town on it.

"Have you made it to Gibson's on the mainland, Kitty?" Elaine asked when I passed her a serving of gelato.

"The antique store? No. Hopefully soon."

Steph put her head on Chris's shoulder, enthusing, "I love Gibson's. They have everything there. Literally every type of antique."

"Kitty's been too occupied with the cottage," Jace reminded them, his affectionate gaze warming me.

"Are we discussing Gibson's?" Jace's sister Candy had returned from changing her baby's diaper in time to hear the last part of Steph's comment. "What are you looking for, Kitty?"

"Jadeite glassware. Mosser manufactured, I think, for my kitchen. There will be display cabinets on either side of the sink." I handed the ice cream scoop to Jace so he could take over serving then dug into my purse for the 3D renderings by Louella at Sendler and Grove.

Steph, Elaine, Andrea, and Candy huddled on the picnic table bench across from me to examine the printouts, oohing and aahing. Andrea said, "Please tell me you're having a housewarming."

Candy added, "And that we're invited!"

I frowned. It hadn't occurred to me to throw a party since I didn't know many people on the island. After visiting the Atlas home twice, I couldn't say that anymore—they'd already made me a de facto family member. "Should I?"

"Why not?" Jace interjected. He placed a bowl and spoon in front of me then brought his thumb to his mouth to flick off a smear of gelato left behind with his tongue. "We're on track to complete the project in August."

Distracted and struck inarticulate by Jace's casual action, I played it off, lifting my soda.

"You absolutely should have a housewarming," Elaine said. "I'll make finger sandwiches."

I could also invite Mitzi. "Alright."

After dessert, Candy's baby became fussy, and she and her husband Mac headed home to get him tucked into bed. Their departure was followed by Jackson and Andrea and their twin daughters.

Elaine announced to those of us remaining, "I DVR'd

Thursday and Friday's *Wheel of Fortune*. Anyone game? Double or nothing?"

"You betcha." Ethan cracked his knuckles as if he were limbering up.

Jace angled toward me, explaining in a hushed voice, "There's currently a fierce competition for who can solve puzzles the fastest. Ma's leading by a hair."

"We're in," Chris replied, and he and Steph stood, gathering dishes and napkins.

Jace's brother Joey unfolded from the picnic bench to cue up the show. He'd been quiet at the Memorial Day barbecue, and I'd assumed it was because of my presence, but Jace told me he was a man of few words. In that sense, Joey was dissimilar from his outgoing family, but he was no doubt an Atlas with his sun-bleached hair, tanned skin, and hazel-flecked green eyes. At the base of the steps leading to the deck, he called, "Penny!"

With a bark, Penny wagged her stubby tail and trotted to Joey's side.

"We'll be there in a minute," Jace said. Everyone filed up the stairs, leaving us alone. Dusk heralded an influx of mosquitoes and chirping crickets. Jace lit a citronella candle, evidence he wasn't in a hurry to join the others. "Shall we switch to the Adirondack chairs by Ma's perennial garden? They're more comfortable than the picnic table bench."

Wishing to prolong his company, I let him guide me to the pair of wooden chairs. Choosing one, I arranged the skirt of my sundress and braced my feet on the matching ottoman.

Jace put the candle on the table between the chairs then flopped into the other chair, sighing. It was a sultry evening, a sleepy breeze stirring. Closing my eyes, I relished the languid mood. I liked that Jace and I could sit without speaking. That it didn't feel odd but companionable.

"I've mulled over what you said, Kitty. About the partnership?"

Eyes fluttering open, I sought Jace's handsome face. The flame flickered, casting the planes of his cheekbones in relief. It lent him an enigmatic quality. I prompted, "And?"

"I'm doing it. I'm gonna approach my family this week."

"Really?"

"The sooner the better," Jace replied. "They'll have to sort out my replacement."

Suddenly alarmed, I straightened. "You're not quitting on me, are you?"

He chuckled. "I wouldn't do that."

"Phew." I slumped against the slatted backrest and fanned my cheeks. "You scared me."

"I'll ride out the year. Winter is All Trade's slowest season, but it's ideal for furniture making. By spring, I'll be doing it full-time."

"When will I see your handiwork?"

"Next weekend, if you want."

"Yes, please," I said.

"You can check out the progress on your table—I've been working on it using your sketch as inspiration."

"You're as much of a workaholic as I am, Jace."

"It's my passion."

"Like real estate is mine." I considered the twilight sky peeking through the canopy of trees. "I'm so blessed. I get to sell dreams."

Jace was gruff when he replied, "I owe you a debt of gratitude, you know."

"Me?" We linked gazes. "How so?"

"It's because of you, my decision. You motivated me. What you shared, the advice you offered."

"It was nothing," I insisted, waving my hand.

"I've noticed how reserved you are about your life. That you aren't a woman who opens up. It means a lot to me that you did." Jace reached to grip my wrist then intertwined our fingers. He leaned across the table, brushing my knuckles with his lips.

I gasped, my body thrumming with an immediate arousal.

"So don't say it was nothing," Jace murmured against my knuckles. "It meant everything—it means everything. You have no idea how much I value your opinion, Kitty."

Tell him who you are. Tell him. Now, before you get mired in any deeper.

"Jace, I—"

The screen door above us squeaked. "Kitty? Jace? Y'all missed the first episode."

"We're comin', Ma." Jace released my hand, his expression regretful. When he stood, he mouthed *sorry*.

CHAPTER TWENTY-ONE

I MAY AS WELL FACE FACTS—I'M FALLING FOR JACE ATLAS.

Did we have a future? Who bloody knew.

Nonetheless, the reality was that with each passing day, I felt further detached from my life in Santa Beatriz and more entrenched in the one I was forging in Kingfisher Cove with Jace. Even if coming clean about my identity dredged up painful memories about my past, we were due for a heart-to-heart ASAP.

Jace arrived Monday morning with his All Trades laborers in tow. He apologized for failing to mention the previous evening that the Cleary Beach contract had concluded. "We'll take advantage of the lull between jobs and focus on Rand-cliffe Cottage."

That week the house became a bustling construction zone. The days were long and hectic, not allowing Jace and me any occasion to be alone together. I endeavored to stay out of the crew's way, wrapping up my final sanding tasks, the veranda and the window frames. Penny supervised me.

On Thursday, the drywalling done, loose ends were tied up—mounting the vintage light fixtures I'd purchased online, installing the built-ins and closet organizers, retrofitting the pantry for a washer-dryer combo, and reglazing window panes.

Mid-morning Friday, I stripped off my N95 mask and my gloves, doing a jig before chucking them into the dumpster. The cottage's exterior was ready for priming, which was on Monday's agenda.

The hardwood flooring was being laid. A table saw was set up in the backyard, the guys accessing it from the parlor or the primary bedroom through either set of French doors. The whir of the saw or the intermittent, rapid-fire noise from a pneumatic nailer became commonplace, garnering dirty looks from my neighbors from where they lazed on the beach behind their rentals.

I walked around the house and poked my head in the parlor. It was a hive of activity. Jace was on his knees in the hallway assembling a staggered pattern with lengths of board. When he noticed me, he got up and came outside.

"I'm driving to the mainland now to test drive that car I showed you on the web yesterday," I told him.

"Want me to tag along?"

"No, not necessary."

He used the back of his hand to wipe away the sweat on his forehead, his manner distracted. "Will you come back here afterward?"

"In all probability, it'll be quite late when I leave the dealership. If the car is in as good of shape in person as online, I'm buying today."

"We're gonna press on, get this floor laid tonight. I'll lock up when we go."

I felt a prang of apprehension. Something was definitely bothering Jace. Had his family reacted poorly to his proposal to cut ties with All Trades? "Until tomorrow then."

SATURDAY AFTERNOON I drove my rental to the airport, Jace trailing me in my new car, a five-year-old silver Volvo wagon.

After returning the rental, I slid into the passenger seat, and Jace pulled from the curb. "How does it handle? Not too shabby, right?"

He tossed me a perfunctory smile. "I approve."

"I should've bought it last month and saved on rental fees," I lamented, scanning my invoice. Yikes. I folded it and stuck it in my purse. "Tell me about the woodshop you're taking me to."

"Clint's place is in the boonies south of Silber Sound. He has a pole barn on his acreage."

My eyebrows rose involuntarily. "Acreage? That's prime real estate out there."

"Woodworking can be a lucrative industry. Clint does well for himself."

He seemed broody during the trip. The atmosphere between us was seldom uneasy, yet I didn't quiz Jace about what ailed him. I'd permit him space. Busying myself with my cell, I scrolled retailers for linens. He'd promised me the cottage would be livable in a week, and I'd already shopped for my bedroom furniture—a mattress, iron headboard, bureau, and side tables.

Exiting the highway, Jace maneuvered the Volvo onto a winding, tree-lined gravel road. We veered left, and a squat ranch-style home surrounded by outbuildings came into view. He parked at the metal structure behind the house.

Inside was cavernous, smelling of varnish and fresh-cut timber. Exposed venting from an HVAC system suspended from the ceiling above us, the joists interspersed with LED fixtures. Pegboard walls along the perimeter held a multitude of unfamiliar tools. There were shelves of glues and stains. Jace played tour guide, pointing out workbenches and planers and joiners. My gaze lasered on furniture in various stages of completion in the far corner of the woodshop. "There it is. You brought my sketch to life."

The top was about fifty inches in diameter, set on a carved pedestal base. "It's how you envisioned it?"

My sketch had been rudimentary in the extreme—a rounded tabletop on a center base—and I'd assured Jace he had full creative license with the design. I ran a hand along the top's beveled edge. "It's better! What kind of wood is this?"

"Oak," he said. "Of course it needs more sandpapering before staining and sealing."

I was in awe of Jace's talent. He was an artisan. Was there anything he couldn't do? "It's beautiful. Truly."

His cheeks pinkened. "Do you want to choose the finish while we're here? I have a brochure with swatches."

I nodded. "I'd like the top stained, but would you be offended if I wanted the pedestal painted instead?"

"I'm not offended." Jace took a booklet from a stack of papers on the shelf above a workbench. He thumbed through the pages then handed it to me. "I'd stay with a tone similar to the floor stain you picked."

I skimmed the options, tapping a swatch. "Forest Cypress."

"Nice. Did you want chairs?" He cautioned, "They might take me a while."

"No, I have my eye on an upholstered set in a floral fabric."

"Well, go ahead and get them shipped. I'll deliver the table next week sometime, after you move into the cottage."

Jace locked the door behind us when we left. During the drive to drop him at his truck, he lapsed into silence again. This time I was compelled to ask, "Are you okay? You haven't been acting like yourself."

He scratched at his scruff, looking doleful. "I'm sorry, Kitty."

"What for?"

"For sulking."

"You aren't. You just seem aloof, which isn't you." I put my hand on his forearm. "What's wrong?"

He sighed. "I broke the news to my family, and Ethan didn't take it so great."

"I worried that was the case," I admitted, waiting for him to elaborate.

"Ma's supportive, but I know she's hiding that she's crushed. Pop would be, too. He wanted All Trades to be his legacy. It was bad enough Jackson and Joey chose to fish." Jace raked a hand through his hair. "Ethan... Ethan's pissed at me. It's like I'm betraying him."

"Maybe his anger stems from a feeling that you're abandoning him," I suggested.

"Could be. He's the face of Atlas, with me as his second in command. When I'm gone, it all rests on his shoulders. It's a lot."

"What about Chris? Can't he pitch in?"

"He likes working alongside the crew. Says he's not suited for management."

"Do you suppose Ethan feels trapped in his role? Maybe *he* stays with the company because of a sense of obligation."

"Shit." Jace pulled a face. "That never occurred to me. I wonder if you're right. You know, if Ethan left, the business would collapse. And that would kill Ma."

"Hey, I'm probably completely off-base," I said. "What do I know? It's more likely you threw him for a loop, and he needs time to digest, to gain perspective. He'll come around, Jace."

"I pray you're right. This whole mess makes me sick."

CHAPTER TWENTY-TWO

THE ALL TRADES LABORERS FINISHED STAINING AND SEALING THE hardwood floors then shifted to outside projects at the close of the following week—the paver patio, pergola, and window boxes. Done in by all the sanding work, I invested in a paint sprayer and gave the siding a cursory coat of primer. On Friday, I applied Haint Blue to the veranda's ceiling. Jace carried on working after the crew departed for the weekend, installing the outdoor fans and lighting. I assisted him, passing him tools on demand.

After, Jace packed his toolbox, looking dog-tired. I was concerned it was the stress of his family issue weighing heavy on him. As night fell, we dawdled at his truck, Penny napping in the passenger seat. He said, "I can't wrap my head around the fact June's almost over."

"Me either. Having the crew here passed time in the blink of an eye."

Yawning, Jace reclined against the hood. "Thanks to them, we're ahead of schedule. In fact, I received an email from Louella yesterday. Your kitchen and bath materials are due for arrival July tenth."

My mouth parted. "*July tenth*? That's only two weeks away!"

"It means I'll be out of your hair earlier than I predicted."

A pang of sadness engulfed me. Before I could ask Jace whether we should continue seeing each other, he confided, "Ethan requested I hold off striking out on my own for another year."

I grasped his work-calloused hand and laced our fingers. "You don't want to do that, do you?"

"No." He laughed tersely. "But I told him I'd mull it over."

Clicking my tongue in sympathy, I tilted my neck, laying my head on his shoulder.

"I haven't been able to sleep—haven't had a solid eight hours in I don't know how long. Damn, Kitty. I hate arguing and disagreements."

"I'm not really a fan either," I replied.

Jace rested his cheek against the crown of my head and exhaled. I felt the tension draining from his body. "Will you be at Sunday supper?"

"Naturally. It's tradition."

Before Jace stepped away to leave, he hugged me. Burying my face in his shirt, I held him tight.

"Talking to you consoles me, Kitty. It always consoles me."

I watched him navigate down Sand Dollar Way then went inside, feeling melancholy. The cottage restoration neared its conclusion, and while Jace and I had a connection, our relationship remained undefined. I didn't care for that. Nope. Uncertainties made me itchy. I favored order. Control. Everything organized in a tidy little box.

My plan seemed clear-cut enough in Santa Beatriz—buy Randcliffe Cottage. Refurbish Randcliffe Cottage. Vacation at Randcliffe Cottage. Period.

Massaging my temples, I shook off my discontent. I wandered from room to room, taking stock. The windows and doors were flung open to dispel the vestiges of wood lacquer fumes, but the floors were worth the odor. They were gorgeous, and once I painted the walls, all that was lacking was décor. Cans of my preferred shades were in the garden shed, along with the housewares I'd amassed.

Pulling my cell from my pocket, I tracked my furniture shipment, confirming it would arrive tomorrow. Tonight would be my last at Shoreside. In the morning I'd check out and move into the cottage. I decided to roll up my sleeves and paint my bedroom now.

SATURDAY, I hung my meager wardrobe in the bedroom closet. The day was devoted to assembling my new bed and bedroom furniture with the drill Jace lent me. I'd selected a shabby chic dresser and side tables in an off-white called Sour Cream and drapes that coordinated with the soft green walls.

It was past my bedtime when I got the rattan window shades installed and arranged the furniture to my liking, the bed facing the French doors so it overlooked the ocean. Bleary-eyed, I sat on the edge of the mattress, unwrapping packages—pillows. A fluffy duvet. Sheets and pillowcases that matched the walls. Shams and duvet cover embroidered in a green and blue pattern.

Once the bed was made, I stood back. I'd taken care to fashion a bedroom befitting a seaside retreat. The color scheme was restful, harmonizing with the blue I'd painted the en suite bath. An area rug, prints for the walls, and a plant would complete the look. I secured the French doors, lowered the shades, and drew the drapes shut before heading to the bathroom.

My body protesting from my exertions, I ran a bath as hot as I could bear, pouring in scented Epsom salts. Soaking in the clawfoot tub alleviated a measure of the pain, and I slept like a rock my first night in Randcliffe Cottage.

I woke stiff and unable to stand straight. Listening to my body, I luxuriated in bed with a book until Sunday supper. Lunch was crackers and an apple.

Shortly before five, when my Uber was due, I dressed in a ruffled blouse, capris, and sandals then waited outside for my ride. Everyone was in attendance at the Atlas house. Chris manned the grill, Ethan lounging beside him, holding a beer by the neck. Joey and Steph brought side dishes from the house. The others sat at a picnic table playing a card game with Jackson and Andrea's twin daughters.

Did I sense forced joviality?

Jace approached me as I placed the pastries I'd bought for dessert on the buffet table, and I spotted him and Ethan exchange terse glances. Smiling brightly, I said, "Looks like taco fixin's. What kind of fish is that on the grill?"

Chris replied over his shoulder, "Snapper, caught today courtesy of Jackson and Joey."

We made our plates, but the mood was strained. Elaine asked me for an update on the cottage, and that drove the conversation during supper.

"I've saved all of this week's episodes of *Wheel*. I thought we could have a marathon," she said.

"Can me and Larissa stay outside and play with Penny, Mama?" Maliyah asked Andrea.

"As long as you stay in the backyard with her. Don't go outside the gate."

Once the table was cleared and the leftovers stowed in the fridge, we congregated in the living room. There weren't enough seats, but Jace insisted I sit on the sofa beside Candy, and he sat on the floor, his back resting against my calf.

I solved two puzzles in a row, and Jace and I high-fived. The game show was a distraction, dulling the friction in the air. Even Ethan got into the spirit and participated, betting me five dollars he'd solve the bonus round before me. We were almost through Wednesday's recording when his phone trilled.

Chris used the remote to pause the DVR, and we listened to Ethan speak to an agitated client, reassuring them help was imminent. Disconnecting the call, he turned to Jace. "Stan at The Shanty. They've got a problem with their pipes. Burst, clogged. He doesn't know, but he's freaking. There's a foot of standing water in their cellar, and they've had to close for the night."

Jace growled, evidently aggravated. "I warned him last time he called for emergency service—I can't keep slapping a Band-aid on his system. It needs substantial, and expensive, revamping."

"He realizes that now," Ethan said. "I guess the crew will be working at Kitty's cottage solo. Who knows how long you're gonna be preoccupied with the job at Stan's bar."

My heart sank.

CHAPTER TWENTY-THREE

Atlas's largest job of the summer launched that week, leaving me with a skeleton crew at the cottage. I wasn't disappointed—everything inside, save the kitchen and hallway bath, was completed. My washer-dryer combo were hooked up. The paver patio had been re-laid. The only remaining projects were the construction of the pergola over the driveway and the window boxes, which the laborers guaranteed would be done before the holiday weekend.

What *did* disappoint me? Jace and Penny's absence. They'd become permanent fixtures at Randcliffe Cottage, and when they weren't around, I felt… incomplete.

Accompanying Jace to the All Trades van Sunday night to see him off, he'd explained he may be forced to assign my kitchen and bath installation to others in the company. With his firsthand knowledge of the horrific plumbing situation at The Shanty, he predicted it would take more than a week's work to sort it out. After finishing there, Jace's presence was required at the new job. He'd be putting in considerable overtime, but he promised to text me.

What else was there to do but put on my big girl panties

and deal with it? I threw myself into my tasks at the cottage—painting, painting, and more painting.

Decorating was the fun part of the renovation, and furniture deliveries were impending, so I elected to paint the interior first. My plan was a room a day, which seemed reasonable enough. I'd researched color palettes before buying paint, building a selection of white, cream, blue, and green tones. It was important to me that rooms flowed and that my décor be cohesive.

Monday, I painted the shiplap walls in the kitchen and pantry white. Tuesday was the dining room, a green. Wednesday, the hallway and foyer in cream then the main bathroom in a saturated blue. Thursday was the guestroom, a blue-green. Friday, I painted the final room—the parlor—a blue called Naval. The color popped against the white built-ins and trim. I'd ordered an oatmeal upholstered sofa and an area rug for the room too, along with side chairs in a blue and green printed fabric.

While waiting for my final coat of Naval to dry in the parlor, I inspected the pergola before the crew packed up for the weekend. They'd worked around the dumpster, which wouldn't be removed until the kitchen and bath were completed. Attached to the cottage on one side, the pergola spanned the width of the driveway, forming a carport of sorts. Chewing my fingernail, I flip-flopped whether to stain it or paint it. If I painted it, it would add uniformity and presence to the overall look of the property.

I settled on paint as my cell alerted me to a message. Pulling it from my pocket, I was pleased it was from Jace.

Miss you. Can't wait to see you Sunday.

Those two sentences breathed fire into me. Brought me to life. I typed out a reply.

I miss you so much, Jace. Randcliffe Cottage isn't the same without you.

I WAS optimistic about the cottage's progress when my Uber driver drove me to Sunday supper on July 3rd. After the holiday, I'd use the sprayer to paint the exterior, then, other than planting flowers, buying furnishings, and decorating, there wasn't much else for me to do but vacation until the kitchen and bathroom were installed.

Now... if only Jace's schedule would slacken, permitting us time to be alone together. In honor of the holiday, I'd bought a navy dress with polka dots, a red purse, and a pair of red sandals. We hadn't seen each other for a week. A week! Bees buzzed in my belly at the thought of Jace's gaze locking on me.

He was on the front porch when I arrived, his hip hitched against the railing. He looked tired but attractive as ever. His faded jeans clung to all the right places, and he had his arms crossed, which highlighted his well-defined biceps.

I grabbed my purse and the cookies I'd purchased from the bakery before alighting from my Uber then hurried down the sidewalk and climbed the porch steps. My heart gathered speed at the sight of him. The welcoming way Jace's eyes lit up made me tingle all over.

It was the most natural thing in the world for me to lift my face to his for a kiss at the top of the stairs.

My eyelids fluttering shut, I inhaled Jace's soapy, clean cologne. Waited. My behavior was bold. Would his lips graze mine? My question was answered a second later when Jace bent his head and kissed me, his movements tentative. Explorative. I moaned. When he deepened the kiss, I returned it. The euphoria injecting my veins was more addictive than any drug.

I'd hesitated to act on our attraction before, but I couldn't deny it any longer. Jace grasped me, hauling me hard against his pelvis. The bakery box tumbled to the floor along with my purse, and I wound my arms around his neck. Tangled my fingers in his hair. My body had begged for this for so long.

Finally, it sang.

Finally.

Jace broke contact, his breathing ragged. He put his forehead to mine then flicked his tongue across my lower lip, rasping against my mouth, "Christ, Kitty."

The sizeable ridge of Jace's arousal poked my belly button. Desire pooled low at my center, thirsting for more. I squirmed against him, and he made a hissing sound. Opening my eyes, I discovered his heavy-lidded gaze on me.

"I told you I missed you," I whispered.

Jace's hands tightened on my waist. "You look incredible."

"So do you." I angled my neck, claiming his mouth. Now that I knew how wonderful kissing him felt, I never wanted to stop.

The screen door screeched. Someone cleared their throat. I dragged myself from Jace, my brain in a dense fog.

Fee stood in the doorway wearing a patterned sundress with a halter-style neckline, her hands on her hips. She leered at us, wiggling her eyebrows. "About time you two came up for air. I was beginning to think I'd have to turn the garden hose on you."

CHAPTER TWENTY-FOUR

I SQUEALED.

Jace released me, saying, "We wanted to surprise you."

"Surprise!" Fee sing-songed, making jazz hands.

I launched myself at my best friend, embracing her. "Did you sell the Weinfarb property?"

"Yes. Then I assigned Jeanine to manage the inspection details, so I'd be free to gallivant."

I pulled away, and we said in unison, "Perk of being the boss."

Laughing, we made our way through the living room, talking a mile a minute. Jace trailed behind us, carrying the bakery box and my purse.

"How long can you stay?"

"'Til Saturday. What do you still need help with at the cottage?"

I ticked the tasks off my fingertips, listing the remaining projects. "Painting the exterior, planting flowers in the window boxes and at the pergola, shopping, and decorating."

Fee pulled a face. "I'd hoped I'd escape the painting."

"I bought a sprayer—it won't take more than a few days if one of us does the trim and the other sprays."

Jace held the kitchen door for us, and we descended the deck steps to the backyard where the family gathered. At our appearance, they clapped and cheered. Elaine asked me, "Were you taken aback when you saw Fiona?"

"You could've knocked me over with a feather." I smiled at the Atlases in turn, touched by their thoughtfulness. "Who's responsible for orchestrating the surprise?"

Ethan said, "I'd mentioned Fiona a while ago, but this was all Jace's doing."

"No," Jace interjected. "It was Ma who floated the idea first. I just called Fiona and coordinated her itinerary. Let's call it a belated birthday gift, Kitty."

How did Jace know about my birthday last month? I hadn't said anything about it, instead celebrating it all by my lonesome with a cupcake after a day's work at the cottage. I looked at Fee.

"Typical Kitty, not wanting anyone to make a fuss." She wagged a finger at me in a scolding way. "Shame on you."

"Not make a fuss? Darn right we're going to make a fuss," Elaine said as she gave me a warm hug.

I smooched Elaine's cheek before pivoting to Jace. Tears swam in my eyes, but I blinked them away. "Thank you so much."

Jace put his arm around my shoulders, bringing me into the crook of his arm. When he kissed the top of my head, realization hit.

I'm in love with this man.

I practically swooned.

I felt Fee's narrowed gaze on me, and I schooled my face. Sure, I'd reckoned I was falling for Jace, but now it was too late. There was no turning back. I was a goner.

Someone put a wine cooler in my palm. Inarticulate, I was steered to a picnic table. Taking a seat at the end of the bench across from Jace and beside Fee, I nursed my drink and listened to her banter with the family. Preoccupied with my thoughts, I attempted to take part in the conversation, but it was futile.

A whine drew my attention. Penny sat on the ground at my feet. She put a paw on my leg. "Hi, baby girl." I stroked the vizsla's velvety ears, imagining her and Jace and me at the cottage. We'd have a meal at the dining room table Jace was making for me, then the three of us would stroll down the beach. I ought to buy her a dog bed for the parlor *and* the bedroom because we'd...

Whoa. You're getting ahead of yourself. Rein it in.

"Kitty?" Jace asked, and I twisted in my seat, facing forward. He squeezed lemon on a platter of oysters on the half shell, indicating I should serve myself.

I declined, but Fee filched one. Before she tipped the shell and slurped, she said suggestively, "Come on, Kit. Some say raw oysters are an aphrodisiac."

My cheeks heating, I caught Ethan's entranced gaze track the motion of Fee's throat as she swallowed the oyster. From the other end of the table, Joey also regarded her with hungry eyes.

Since I didn't have a guest bed yet, Fee shared mine that night. I woke on Monday to her flinging the French doors open. Squinting, I sat up and rubbed my eyes.

Fee stood on the patio in her pajamas. The sun hit the highlights in her hair as she looked around. "This place is shaping up, but you know what you need, Kit?"

"I have the sneaking suspicion you're about to inform me," I said, my voice hoarse from slumber. I picked up my phone from my bedside table, squinting at the screen. 7:35 a.m. "Geez, do we have to wake up this early?"

She persisted as if I hadn't spoken, "You need those wooden chairs like Elaine has in her backyard, for down by the shore—"

"Adirondack chairs," I supplied.

"Yeah, those. And a gas grill for the patio, so we can cook out while I'm visiting." She spun on her heel and strode inside. "And a table and chair set with an umbrella."

"I was going to buy all that next season," I said, swinging my legs over the edge of the mattress and planting my feet on the floor. "My bank balance is abysmal. I'm blowing through my savings at an alarming rate."

Fee plopped on the bed beside me, saying breezily, "You only live once."

I didn't respond.

"That account was earmarked for the cottage. Expenditures are part of the plan—it's not impulsivity," she reminded me. "I know you're fretting, but you aren't spinning out of control, Kit. You aren't your grandfather."

"Uh, may I remind you of the numerous sessions I had with a psychiatrist in my twenties?" I asked. "I know how to cope with my anxiety with money these days. It's only that I've gone over budget for this year with buying the Volvo. I need to cool it for a while."

Fee bumped her shoulder into mine. "Then you'll be tickled pink because I intend to purchase the outdoor stuff for you as a housewarming gift. I will, however, allow you to buy me breakfast before I do."

"We should be painting today," I grumbled half-heartedly.

"Ethan said to bring folding chairs and a beverage cooler for the fireworks display at Cleary Beach later. You don't have either."

"No, I don't."

"So we have to run to the store regardless."

"I suppose. But I wanted to drop by Mitzi's before we went to the beach, to introduce you."

"We can always do that tomorrow evening if we don't have time today." Fee got up, kneeling to root through her suitcase pushed against the wall beside my dresser. She unearthed a slightly wrinkled Kelly green sundress. "Will you bust a move already? Restaurants will be crazy today with it being the Fourth."

"Fine." I stood and stretched. Edelweiss Café on the mainland just over the bridge made a tasty egg and cheese croissant sandwich with a side of homemade granola. I'd treat Fee to breakfast there since the stores we'd be visiting were on the mainland. "We absolutely have to spend *all day* painting tomorrow."

Fee mock-saluted me. "Yes, Drill Master!"

CHAPTER TWENTY-FIVE

THE STREETS WERE BLOCKED OFF FROM THE PARADE EARLIER THAT day, so our Uber driver dropped us several blocks from Cleary Beach.

We hoofed it to the boardwalk, lugging the cooler between us, the bags containing our folding canvas chairs slung over our shoulders. It was hot, the air perfumed with a bouquet of coconut sunblock and buttered popcorn. Crowds of people pressed against us, creating an obstacle course we had to fight our way through. The cooler's handles dug into our palms. We kept having to set it down.

Fee projected her voice over the live music blasting from the band shell further down the beach. "Tell me again why we're here with the peasants instead of at Shoreside enjoying a genteel pre-fireworks cocktail."

"Only club members and guests staying at Shoreside are invited, and they jack their rates sky-high during the holiday." I wore a black maillot on the off-chance we wanted to swim, a knee-length black-and-white coverup over it, and my espadrilles. Sweat trickled down my spine. I blew a raspberry, feeling harried. "Although a mint julep at The Seafarer sounds damn tempting right about now."

"Amen to that," Fee mumbled. Her hair was frizzed from the humidity, her face flushed and beaded with sweat. "Hold up. My strap is falling."

"Who knew ice and soda would be so heavy." We sat the cooler on the ground. People flowed around us. I flexed my fingers, wincing. Fee slipped a hand through the neckline of her filmy white caftan, adjusting the strap of her tropical-print bikini. When we resumed our journey, I acknowledged, "In hindsight, maybe we should've stayed at the cottage. But you seemed gung ho about watching the fireworks with the Atlases last night."

"I was, as you were." She gave me side-eye as we staggered down the boardwalk to our meetup spot, asking slyly, "You dying to see your lover boy?"

"Don't start that again." All afternoon I'd fielded naughty questions about me and Jace.

"I saw the way he was devouring you with those bedroom eyes. If you two had been alone, he would've splayed you over the picnic table and had his wicked way with you."

Picturing it, a shiver coursed through me. Instead of replying, I teased, "Sure, Scarlett."

Fee's brow creased. "Huh?"

"You were Scarlett O'Hara last night, with Joey and Ethan as the Tarleton twins tripping and slobbering all over themselves to fix you a supper plate." I made a gagging gesture. "Eww."

Fee doubled over with laughter, almost losing her grip on the cooler. "Fiddle-dee-dee, Kitty."

I giggled, then sobering, I said, "Keep an eye out. The Atlases are around here somewhere." I heard a sharp whistle and halted, searching the crowds on the beach. Jace waved at us. He was in swim trunks, and his hair was wet, a towel around his shoulders.

"Thank God," Fee breathed. We headed to the nearest flight of wooden stairs granting beach access.

Joey and Jace jogged to meet us mid-step, taking the cooler and our bags with the canvas chairs. Fee and I sagged with relief, our enthusiasm rallying. The family was set up by the water on blankets and folding chairs, surrounded by coolers. Calling out welcomes, they entreated us to sit. I grabbed colas from our cooler for Fee and me then sank to the blanket beside Jace. Elaine enquired about what we'd been up to that morning, and Fee filled them in about our shopping trip.

I said, "We were able to fit the chairs and grill into the wagon, so we'll be putting those together this week."

Fee swallowed a drink of soda. "The patio set won't be delivered until after I've gone home, unfortunately."

"No, but I'll have it in time for the housewarming," I replied.

Candy and Mac arrived minutes later, encumbered with baby Eddie, his diaper bag, two chairs, a cooler, and an umbrella. Mac set the cooler down then stuck the umbrella in the sand and cranked it open. Jace and I were thrown into shadow.

Candy explained as she wrestled with a folding chair while holding her son, "It's always a hassle schlepping the umbrella, but the afternoon sun is fierce."

"Here," I said, extending my arms. "I'll take the baby."

Candy handed him off. "Thanks. Can you keep him while I use the restroom?"

At my nod, Candy hastened across the sand to the public bathrooms. The sleeping baby was jiggly, which I found awkward—I had zero experience with newborns. I'd only offered to hold him out of obligation.

"Eddie's named after my Pop," Jace said, studying me.

Cradling the baby against my bosom, I supported his floppy head. Jackson and Andrea's twins sprinted up to us, dripping seawater and shouting, "Yay! Eddie's here."

Jace shushed them. "Let him nap, girls."

"The fireworks will wake him up, if he sleeps that long,"

Maliyah said. "Aunt Candy says if he gets scared, they'll go home."

Larissa told me, "Penny always gets scared. She's in her crate at Grandma's."

Maliyah yanked Larissa's arm. "I want to swim again, sissy."

They tore off, kicking up sand we had to dodge. Jace leaned close and put his lips to my ear, whispering. "You're quiet today, Kitty. Are you regretting our kiss?"

Regret it? No. I wanted more. Turning my head, I met his gaze and whispered back, "I wish we could sneak off and be by ourselves."

Jace threw me a sexy grin. "Leave it to me."

When Candy returned from the restroom and retrieved Eddie, Jace asked if I'd like to go into the water with him. He got up, holding out a hand. I stripped off my coverup, not noticing the swarms of beachgoers around us, their conversations, or the music pumping from the band shell.

There was only Jace.

Normally, I'd feel self-conscious, but the way Jace's sizzling gaze roved my bare flesh showed me he liked what he saw. My heart banged like a drum, the adrenaline infusing my bloodstream, making me dizzy and rubber-legged. Clasping my hand, he led me into the surf. Wordlessly, we waded into deeper water, distancing from the other swimmers.

"We're far away enough to have privacy. We've gotta be careful though—sound carries further than on land," Jace said in a hushed tone, pulling me to him. Our chests made contact, and my nipples pebbled.

Breathless, I caressed his face. "I don't know what got into me yesterday, but I'm glad we kissed."

"So am I. You're all I can think about." His nostrils flared, and he nuzzled his cheek against my hand.

"I don't want to waste the rest of this summer."

"We won't." Cupping my backside, Jace hefted me so we were pelvis to pelvis, his arousal jutting. "Since our kiss," he confided thickly, putting his lips on my collarbone, "I've had to jerk off three times."

Jace's words set my senses humming. "What if people see us?"

He shifted so he faced away from the beach, shielding me from view. My fingers gripping his shoulders, I shut my eyes and tipped my head. Jace bit and suckled the curve of my neck, his tongue swirling over my clavicle and the hollow between my breasts, his whiskers chafing the tender skin there.

One hand underneath me to support me, Jace snaked his other up my ribcage. He located a puckered nipple through my swimsuit, rolling it between his fingers. When he tweaked it, electric desire zapped to my center.

I mewled, seeking his lips. The throbbing ache at my core pleaded for attention. For release. We kissed, our tongues entwining, and I undulated my hips, bucking against his tip. How easy it would be, I thought, for Jace to pull his trunks down… to ruck my bathing suit aside. To penetrate my folds and enter me.

He was girthy, but I was greedy.

"I've waited for this moment—to be able to touch you," Jace panted, gliding a palm slowly down my navel. At the apex of my thighs, he found the elastic edge of my suit, slipping a digit under it. He fondled my mound. "I wonder if I can make you come," he mused, dipping his finger into my slit. "I think I can."

I wrapped my arms around him, tucking my face in his neck. Clenching my thighs, I prodded him with my hips, encouraging him. "Please."

Making a growling noise low in his throat, Jace didn't penetrate me further. Instead he stroked me, teasing me with the pads of his fingers. He found my swollen clit, working it with his thumb, his pace leisurely. "You feel so good."

Exquisite tension built in my core, my heartbeat a roar in my ears. He dipped a finger into my folds, then another, increasing the pressure on my clit with his thumb. I was close. So so close. Thrusting against Jace, I chased the rush. My muscles clenched, and I cried out as spasms of pleasure radiated in surges.

CHAPTER TWENTY-SIX

"The word on the street is Nelson Thibodeux's jamming his clam in his sister-in-law Beulah Worthington," Fee intoned as she scanned the newspaper. "There's—no, this is last week's edition, there *was*—bible study Thursday at the church. Not as riveting. Oh, yum. The mayor's wife is sharing her coconut cake recipe. Ugh, the things I'd do for a slice of cake right now."

"Jamming his clam?" I cackled. "That's a euphemism I haven't heard before."

"According to their masthead, *The Cove Observer* features all the island's latest breaking gossip. Weren't you aware? Bless your heart, Kitty Landis."

"Nobody would pay for that rag—that's why they have to give it away." I balled up my sandwich wrapper, an eye on a loitering seagull. "You better take your last bite before that gull swoops in and steals it. Besides, lunch break is over. We gotta get back to gardening."

Fee groaned, setting the two-page newspaper aside. "We've been so busy I haven't even had a chance to do my Kegels."

"Multi-tasking is a thing," I said dryly and got to my feet.

"Once we plant the flowers in the window boxes, we can have our baths and drive to that antique store everyone raves about on the mainland."

"Oooh. Can we stop for a bite to eat, too?" Fee put her hands together to mime praying. "A woman can't subsist on pretzels and grab 'n go sandwiches alone, babe."

"I thought I'd nip into the supermarket so we can use that fancy grill you bought me. We'll dine on fine china this evening."

"Paper plates?"

"And circle gets the square."

It was Thursday afternoon, and we'd hustled to finish painting the cottage the previous night. Yardwork was on today's schedule, and we'd already mowed, raked beds, weeded, and transplanted the Carolina Jessamine near the driveway pergola. Some much needed relaxation was in order —I hoped Mitzi was up to a visit this evening. She hadn't been all week.

Fee poured potting soil in the window boxes mounted on the veranda railings, and I came behind to fill them with asparagus ferns and tuberous begonias in peaches, pinks, and yellows. After I gave them a soak with the watering can I'd bought at the plant nursery, we stood in the front yard, taking measure of the property.

I shook my head in awe, my chest swelling with pride. The lawn was flawlessly manicured, the landscaping verdant, and the fresh-painted siding glistened in the sunshine. Pink flower beds on either side of the brick steps were a haven for honeybees and butterflies. Yesterday I'd affixed an embossed metal plaque next to the door—Randcliffe Cottage, Est. 1902. "It's charming. And it looks neat as a pin."

"Fantastic curb appeal," Fee agreed. "The pergola makes the cottage even grander. Are you going with wicker furniture for the veranda?"

"No, I want rocking chairs like Elaine Atlas has on hers, eventually."

Belted Kingfishers congregating on my neighbor's fence took wing, preceding the hiss of brakes punctuating the air. I whirled to discover a truck parked in the street. Whooping, I told Fee, "My kitchen and bathroom are here early! I have to text Jace."

I tapped a message to him while the driver unloaded the truck, stacking crates and boxes in the dining room with the other deliveries I'd received. Jace had been occupied with The Shanty, and I'd been occupied with Fee's visit and working on the cottage, but we texted every morning upon waking and every night before bed.

He replied a couple minutes later. *I meant to give you a heads-up. I got an email from Louella the other day, but I've been swamped and forgot. Ethan and I aren't on speaking terms since I broke it to him that I'm not staying another year at All Trades. I'll text him and ask if he'll send a crew over tomorrow.*

Oh, no, I thought. *I've been hoping you and Ethan would patch things up. Sorry. I know how rough that has to be on you.*

Shit happens… depending on how many guys he can spare, everything could be installed by the middle of August.

Will your calendar clear a little by then?

Yes, ma'am. Maybe by as soon as next week sometime. I've got Sunday off, and I want to bring your table. That alright?

My heart constricted, a shiver of excitement tickling the base of my spine. *Very alright. I miss you.*

I miss you.

I sent a kiss emoji, contemplating a risqué text.

"Woolgatherin'?"

I jumped at Fee's query, my cheeks flooding with color as I realized she'd ushered the driver out and bolted the door. If she learned about the indecent thoughts I was having about Jace, I'd never live it down.

"Never mind. I'm off to bathe," she said, her mouth twitching with humor. She swept past me and down the hall.

GIBSON'S ANTIQUE Emporium was housed in a historic three-story brick building taking up a city block, a parking garage beneath it. Regal marble lions stood as sentries at the entrance, and when we stepped over the threshold, an attendant greeted us. She offered us each a wheeled cart reminiscent of an old-fashioned bellman's luggage trolley.

Eyebrows leaping to her hairline, Fee asked, "You really think we need our own carts?"

With a knowing smile, the attendant nodded and handed us self-stick labels with *Sold* in bold letters. "For big-ticket items. Inquire about our freight policy at checkout. Happy shopping."

The first floor was dedicated to all types of furniture. By the time we entered the elevator to convey us to the second level, I'd placed labels on a number of pieces—a black wrought iron bedstead, side tables, lamps, and dresser for the guestroom, an oversized trunk to use as a coffee table in the parlor, a record player and a handful of vinyl records, and a round rope-edged mirror for the hallway.

I wasn't a person who typically enjoyed shopping, but the hunt for treasures fired me up. I piled hand towels on top of a quilt for the guest bed as well as assorted throw pillows. We soldiered on, accumulating an assortment of nautical-inspired tchotchkes, wall art, and rugs.

Glass was on the third floor. A display of Jadeite had me smitten. "These prices are super reasonable. How many should I get for each cabinet?" I asked Fee. "I want to start a collection, not cram it full right away."

"Do an odd amount—like three." Fee picked up a cake

stand. "This is cute and…" she upended it, "a bargain at sixty bucks."

My rolling cart was packed. Fee put the cake stand on her cart. I added a pitcher, two bowls of varied dimensions, a vase, and a butter dish, saying, "I'm terrified to see what the total is. Let's cash out, arrange shipping for the big stuff, and drive to the supermarket."

Once back at the cottage, we unloaded my purchases, then we went out to the patio. Fee suggested, "Why don't we drag the Adirondack chairs up here to by the barbecue?"

"Hello, Kitty!" Mitzi was on her way to her wicker rocker, supported by her walker with Brenda behind her, her grip on the gate belt around Mitzi's hips.

"Oh, good. Mitzi must be on the mend." I called, "Cocktails?"

"You bet. Come on over, gals."

"You weren't kidding about Mitzi's head-to-toe violet," Fee said under her breath as we picked across the neighbor's lawn between Mitzi's property and mine. "Isn't she a fashion plate in that pantsuit!"

"See what you think about her irises. I find them mesmerizing."

When we reached her, Mitzi was settled in her seat. There were bags under her eyes, and her complexion was wan, but her manner was energetic. After Brenda arranged two other rockers beside hers, Mitzi instructed, "Pop a squat."

Brenda went inside to mix our drinks. Fee sat, crossing her legs. I did the same, saying, "You look good, Mitzi. Feeling better?"

"Pfft." Mitzi waved a dismissive hand. "Don't fib. I look like hell, and I'm well aware of that actuality, doll. Barely fit to receive guests. However, I couldn't put off meeting your friend any longer."

After I made the formal introductions, I could tell Fee was as charmed by Mitzi as I was.

"Aren't you a fetching thing. Most ladies with your hair color wouldn't choose outfits in loud patterns like that, but it suits you," Mitzi said, sizing Fee up. She patted her hair, which was piled on the top of her head in a bun. "Mine was once reddish, like yours, until I dyed it this lavender shade."

"I'm obsessed with your outfit. I love fashion," Fee replied, warming up to one of her favorite subjects. "I buy so many clothes that I had to convert my guestroom in my condo into a closet."

They compared the merits of chiffon over georgette until Brenda came from the cottage with a tray. She handed out the drinks before leaving again.

"The famed Mauve Madness. Let me try." Fee sipped. "Grapefruit? I didn't expect that. Yummy. I was wondering, Mitzi, since you knew the Randcliffes back in the day… do you remember Kitty when she was little?"

"Oh, yes, I saw her out and about with Frances and Charlie. This was after Helena and her husband passed, of course. Helena had the wanderlust. Would've followed that fella to the ends of the globe. Hmm, this just isn't agreeing with me today." Mitzi pulled a face, setting her drink down. "Helena's death was challenging for them both, you see, but it changed Frances in many ways. Hardened her."

My eyes filled with unexpected tears at my mother's mention. It wasn't the first time Mitzi had talked about her, but she'd never mentioned her death and its effect on my grandparents before. I swallowed my tears. "I was too young to remember much about my mom. We didn't discuss her."

"It was taxing for Frances and Charlie, I'd wager," Mitzi replied, her expression kind. She sighed, shrinking into her chair. "Taxing for you as well. Although I make a point to speak of Anson—it helps keep him alive for me—I didn't intend to distress you. I apologize, honey."

Fee coughed then changed the subject, asking, "Are you feeling tired, Mitzi? We don't want to wear you out."

"It seems I spend half my life under the weather. If it's not something, it's another," Mitzi said with a careless shrug. "Don't trouble yourself. Kitty, I was thinking earlier today about coming upon Charlie teaching you to golf at Shoreside. He was so patient with you. You must've been what? Nine? Ten?"

"Sounds right." A specter of a smile lifted the corners of my mouth. "I was a klutz. I never mastered the game, even with lessons with the golf pro in my teens."

"Anson and I spent many an afternoon on the links. Charlie doted on you. Of course, you were the spitting image of his beloved Helena."

Fee and I listened to Mitzi's stories about Shoreside in the olden days, her words tugging at my heartstrings. When I noticed her fading, I got up and knocked on the cottage's back door, requesting Brenda assist Mitzi inside. After bidding them goodbye, Fee and I headed back to my place.

"I want to be Mitzi Armbruster when I grow up," Fee enthused as she mixed a bagged salad in a plastic bowl. "What a terrific lady."

"A force of nature," I agreed, "yet extremely frail." I was pensive as I cooked chicken on the grill. My bestie's visit had sailed by, and with her flight leaving mid-morning Saturday, there was scant time for much else except decorating tomorrow. That meant that I needed to discuss something with Fee now, something I'd been pondering for weeks.

When we sat with our plates on our knees, I took a fortifying breath. "Fee? Can we talk?"

CHAPTER TWENTY-SEVEN

FRIDAY, AN ALL TRADES CREW OF THREE MEN SHOWED UP AT THE cottage. Two assembled the lower kitchen cabinets, the third installing the tub in the hallway bathroom. Fee and I hung curtains and blinds and wall art.

I took Fee to the airport Saturday morning then detoured to Save-a-Bunch for cleaning supplies before continuing home. My living room furniture was due between two and five, and I was keen to clean before then.

Sand Dollar Way was alive with the noise of holidaymakers. I dusted and swept the cottage, serenaded by children's laughter from the backyards of neighboring homes. After scrubbing the en suite bathroom, I glanced at the clock, relieved there was time for a bath.

Bathed and dressed, I sat on the veranda with a book, my back to the siding, waiting for the delivery truck. It showed at four. I tipped the driver a twenty, and he helped me arrange the furniture in the parlor before continuing his deliveries.

My stomach demanded sustenance. A quick trip to the butcher shop by Cleary Beach netted me skewers of cubed veggies and steak. While grilling, I plugged my record player into a parlor socket and chose an Etta James LP. When soulful, bluesy "Misty Blue" began, I closed my eyes and moved my hips.

Arms circled my waist, dragging me against a solid chest. I gasped. Stiffened. Once I placed Jace's familiar soapy scent, I wilted against him. He nestled his face into the curve of my neck and chuckled. My body was in tune with his as we swayed from side to side to the music. We fit together as if made for each other—where I was soft and pliant, he was hard and muscled.

I reached up, burying my fingers in his hair. "Mmm. This is lovely."

When the song ended, Jace kissed my ear. "I never want to let you go," he said, his arms reflexively tightening around my waist, "but I brought you something."

"The table?"

"Naw. That'll be another day. C'mon."

I switched off the grill burners. "I'm all yours."

Our fingers interlocked, I accompanied Jace to his Ram. Two rocking chairs were strapped into the truck bed. "Housewarming present," he said with a smile. "They're like Ma's. You said you wanted a pair but in black."

"I did say that. How thoughtful." Tears pooled in my eyes, and I hugged him. "Thank you, Jace."

He returned my embrace, suggesting we put the rockers on the veranda. Once they were in position, I ran a hand over the slatted backrest of the one nearest me. "You made these, didn't you?"

"Guilty."

Sitting, I tested the rocker. Smooth. Fluid. The seat was contoured for comfort. Again, I was struck by Jace's talent, his skills as a craftsman. "These chairs are an excellent gift… How may I show you my appreciation?"

He quirked a brow, giving me a lopsided grin.

So that's what Fee refers to when she says bedroom eyes, I

thought. The primal glint in his gaze ignited me. I squirmed at the promise I found there.

Jace held out a hand. When I got up, he hoisted me over his shoulder. Shrieking, I told him to set me down. He ignored me, unlatching the front door and elbowing it open then kicking it shut behind us. He carried me through the foyer and the hall to my bed. Depositing me on my pillows, he leaned down and unlaced his boots.

Dizzy with desire, I watched Jace undress. The throbbing ache between my thighs was in concert with my heartbeat. Would my heart crash through my ribcage? It was a distinct possibility.

Jace shucked his jeans, then he yanked his boxer briefs down. His cock sprang free. My eyes widened. Wow. A predatory smirk on Jace's face, he approached the bed, crooking a finger to command I sit up. Under his spell, I complied.

He pulled my sundress over my head. When I moved to touch him, he stilled me. Unclasping my bra, Jace removed it, tossing it across the bedroom. A shaft of setting sun beamed through the window, sparking on the wiry hairs on his finely corded, muscular thighs. The sight hypnotized me. I itched to glide my nails over him, to feel the supple strength of his flanks. To wrap my fingers around the silken rigidity of his shaft.

Planting a palm on my sternum, Jace pushed me until I was supine on the bed. He licked his lips. His searing green gaze floated over me. It branded me, leaving my body ablaze. I shivered, my fingers trembling as I tried to shimmy from my panties. Jace hooked his thumbs under the elastic, hitching them from my hips. With the flick of his wrist, the panties joined the bra in the corner of the room.

Placing a knee on the bed between my thighs, Jace nudged until I spread them, then he lay on top of me. I drew a quick breath when his scorching flesh met mine. My body begged for satiation. I bowed my spine and bucked my pelvis—the waiting was sweet torture. Laughing softly, Jace shook his head. "Not yet."

Gathering my wrists together in one hand, he caged my arms over my head. Kissed me thoroughly before moving his mouth to my breasts. He swirled his tongue against each rosy peak, working his way downward to my ribcage then to my navel. Jace paused when he reached the apex of my thighs, only then releasing my hands. I tangled my fingers in his hair, his name on my lips.

Jace splayed my legs further apart. His hooded gaze met mine when he teased the tip of his tongue against my swollen, sensitive nub. Panting, I arched, but he restrained my legs against the mattress with his forearms. Tortured me by methodically laving my lips, then circling and sucking my clit.

I homed in on the frenzied, toe-curling tension building in my center. With a shudder, I went over the edge.

As I came back to earth, Jace positioned himself between my thighs, hovering over me with his arms bracketing my head. He kissed my forehead, my cheeks, my mouth. "My God, Kitty. Every inch of you is perfection."

I was out of breath, my limbs languid and heavy, yet I hungered for more. To feel Jace inside me. I skimmed my palms up the back of his legs, the curve of his spine, traced the length of his back. His cock jerked against my thigh, and I gyrated, urging him.

Lining himself at my entrance, Jace plunged through my folds until he was fully sheathed. He set a deliberate rhythm, his mouth on mine as he flexed his hips, his strokes deep. I got the sense he was restraining himself. His skin was sheened, slick with sweat, his face in my neck. The friction of our bodies was fiery—would we burst into flames? I bit his shoulder, reveling in his salty taste.

Clamping my muscles around him, I cupped his ass and pleaded, "Faster."

Jace moaned hoarsely in answer to my encouragement, increasing the pace of his thrusts. Then, he swelled, stretching me. Euphoric, I flung my head back against the pillows, surrendering to the quickening of pleasure at my center. With a guttural sound, Jace tensed and followed, spilling his seed.

CHAPTER TWENTY-EIGHT

I WOKE TO MORNING SUN STREAMING INTO THE BEDROOM.

Rubbing my eyes, I stretched, my muscles blissfully sore. My stomach growled from hunger, but I felt amazing. Sweeping a hand across the mattress, I searched for Jace, but he wasn't there. He must've gone out to grab us breakfast.

Reclining against my pillows, I laced my hands over my midsection, thoughtful. Jace mentioned the other day that he had Sunday off. That left us free the entire day, until Sunday supper. We had a lot to discuss, not least of which what I'd talked to Fee about. Thankfully, she always had my back—there were major changes coming in my life, and I crossed my fingers that Jace would be by my side.

My reverie was broken by the sound of the kitchen door slamming. I finger-combed my hair then straightened the duvet over my chest. Jace's footsteps echoed in the silence of the cottage. When he appeared in the doorway, I smiled in welcome. His pained expression had me sitting up and putting my feet to the floor. Something was bad wrong. Icy tendrils of dread clamped down on my gut. "What is it?

Jace shook his head, his face chalky. My gaze fell to his hands. He held a take-out drink tray with two coffees and a small bag in one hand. A copy of *The Cove Observer* was clutched in the other. Jace lobbed the paper at me. I caught it before it landed on the floor.

Bringing the paper up, I scanned it, my mouth dropping at the words screaming in bold script across the front page *Blue-Blood Heiress Returns to Ancestral Home, Dalliances with Blue-Collar Boy Toy.* A fuzzy picture of Jace and me canoodling at Cleary Beach was under the lurid byline.

Oh no. Oh no. My head swam. I put a palm to my forehead, wondering if I'd faint. The newspaper fluttered to my feet. "I-I…"

"Is it true? *You're* Katrina Randcliffe?" he asked gruffly.

"Yeah, but—"

Jace's jaw ticked. "The Katrina I met at Hollby Lighthouse fifteen years ago… that was you, right?"

"I—" I tried swallowing away the lump in my throat.

"And you know who I am? You've known… all summer? What the hell? What kind of sick game have you been playing?"

The raw agony on Jace's face tore at me. I got up, extending a hand toward him, but he recoiled from my touch. "I tried to tell you, Jace, but—"

"Bullshit."

"Look, I don't know what that so-called journalist wrote, but they don't know *anything* about me—"

"And neither do I, apparently." Jace gripped the nape of his neck, shaking his head. "The headline says it all—I'm the blue-collar boy toy, and you're the blue-blooded heiress. What the fuck was I thinking?"

Frustration welling, I implored, "Will you calm down and listen to me?"

"Face the facts, *Ms. Randcliffe*," he said my name with scorn, "this would've fizzled out once you went back to Santa Beatriz anyway."

"Let me explain, will you?" I argued, stamping my foot. "It's not fair—"

"What's not fair is messing with my emotions. Misleading me. I'm pissed, and I'm hurt." Jace put a palm up, but the anger drained from him, leaving him looking defeated. Stiff-voiced, he muttered, "I'm out."

"What does that mean?"

"It means I've had enough. I'm out."

"So you're breaking up with me?" I demanded. "You're throwing it all away because of an idiotic newspaper headline?"

"There's a reason Upper King doesn't fraternize with Lower King. We're different breeds. What do we really have in common anyway?" The words were said with no acrimony, only acceptance. He set the tray of coffee on my bedside table. "I'll have one of my guys drop your table by as we won't be seeing each other again before you go home. Have a good life, Katrina."

I trailed him down the hall, indifferent to my nudity. "That's it? You're not going to allow me to defend myself? To make amends?"

Jace walked from the cottage and out of my life.

"A PALTRY FIFTEEN MINUTES," I bawled, "is all it took to end it. Everything I thought we'd built, and—poof—it's gone after a fifteen-minute conversation. He was so cold to me, too. He acted like he hated me."

"Aww, Kit. I'm sorry, babe," Fee tsked over speakerphone. "You want to come home? I'll book you a flight today."

"I can't leave. They just started the kitchen." I blew my nose, feeling morose. "I don't know what to do with myself. It's five o'clock Sunday. I usually go to the Atlases at five on Sundays. I'm on my own again."

"You should reconsider what we spoke about and return to your life in Santa Beatriz once the cottage is renovated."

"And then what? No, I have to stick it out… I meant it when I told you the Cove is my home now. I don't want to leave, even if being here is an excruciating reminder of Jace." Falling silent, my gaze panned the horizon, seeking solace as a trade wind ruffled my hair.

"It's a shame he saw that newspaper exposé before you could tell him who you are," Fee lamented. "Did you read the article? What did it say?"

I scoffed, my throat cracking from all the tears I'd shed, "Article? What article? The headline basically *was* the story. There were three sentences under the picture about me jetting to the island to throw my money around after buying Rand-cliffe Cottage. Whatever hack wrote it didn't even bother researching because, obviously, I'm not an heiress. Not anymore."

"And Jace is supposed to be your—what was it? Your *boy toy*?" Fee snorted. "You gotta give the writer props. They know how to craft a spicy turn of phrase."

"Well, Jace seemed pretty insulted by it," I said tartly.

"Most men would be. They can be thin-skinned creatures."

I put my head in my hands. "I'm hardly thrilled by the notoriety, either. Boy, do I empathize with Beulah Worthington right about now."

"Oh, I forgot about poor Beulah. We shouldn't have laughed about her predicament. Karma rears its ugly head."

"I don't know if her feelings about her brother-in-law are genuine, but mine are for Jace. And I did intend to reveal my identity—I was picking my moment. First, we were never alone. Then when we were, the mood wasn't right. He and Ethan were feuding. There was the emergency job at the bar…" Groaning, I swiped my tissue across my nose. "Today was earmarked for 'the talk'. I swear."

"It's rotten timing."

"God, the connection we had last night. Fee, I've never felt that way before." I confessed, "I love him."

"I realize that, babe, yet it's likely he doesn't. Men aren't always the swiftest when it comes to love."

"He read the text I sent saying we needed to talk but didn't answer." A tear gathered on my waterline. I blinked it away. "Advice, please."

"If he chooses to hear you out, fantastic. Maybe it'll work out between you two. Maybe not. Regardless, you do what we discussed, even if he won't hear you out. You finish renovating the cottage. You make it a real home. Study for your brokerage licensure. Find office space to lease and take your exams. Then you open a branch of Landis-Philips Agency on Kingfisher Cove." Fee took a deep breath. "You move on with your life, like you always have when things fall apart."

"Why do people alway leave me, Fee? What is it about me that makes them want to leave?"

"Oh, sweetie. Don't."

"Jace. My parents—" A knock sounded at the kitchen door, and I started, hope leaping. What if it was Jace? "Someone's here. I'll call you later, okay?"

"Kit?"

I hung up. After blowing my nose again, I ran my hand through my hair then hurried to the kitchen. When I flung the door open, I was flabbergasted to find Brenda on the step, a newspaper tucked under her arm. She caught sight of my swollen eyes and tear-stained face and grimaced.

"Oh, no," she said, her voice contrite. "You've been crying, Kitty."

I frowned, brushing away the moisture on my cheeks and straightening my pajama top.

"You must've read today's edition of *The Cove Observer*." Stumbling over her words, she blubbered, "It's all my fault.

I'm terribly sorry. I don't blame you if you're furious—Ms. Mitzi went ballistic on me when she saw it."

"What?"

"When I brought Ms. Mitzi the paper this afternoon, and she saw the photo, she asked me if I'd told anyone you were a Randcliffe," Brenda explained, studying her tennis shoes. "I didn't know you wanted things hush-hush..."

Welp. That explained it. She was why my life was now in tatters.

My temper flaring, I demanded, "You tipped off the newspaper?"

"Tipped off?" Brenda's face turned stark white. "I-it wasn't like that. Not at all. God as my witness. I may have mentioned you came back to the island to refurbish the family cottage when I was checking out at the supermarket a couple weeks ago... or maybe at O'Flaherty's last month."

"And that tidbit of info spread like wildfire, right?" I snapped. I'd forgotten how household staff tended to melt into the woodwork, enabling them to effortlessly eavesdrop on every conversation. I was a damn fool. "How dare you violate my privacy! You know the island can be a rumor mill, Brenda. Why would you gossip about me?"

Now she was near tears. "Oh, dear, I never meant... it wasn't idle gossip. I meant no harm, Kitty."

It was ironic that all it had taken to ruin what Jace and I had been building was a thoughtless remark to the wrong person. I rubbed my forehead, feeling defeated. All the fight in me ebbed away, and I was left emotionless. Detached.

Brenda stood on the steps, looking pitiful while waiting for me to speak. I couldn't. Shoulders slumping, I shut the door and locked it.

CHAPTER TWENTY-NINE

ANY OPTIMISM I POSSESSED FADED BY DEGREES, DESPONDENCY taking its place when Jace failed to respond to my text. I'd convinced myself that once he cooled off, he'd regain his level-headed demeanor. That he'd reach out, demand an explanation.

He didn't.

By the middle of August, the kitchen and bath projects wrapped. Jace sent someone to complete the remaining plumbing work. Another crew member delivered my dining table.

After Brenda's appearance at my door, I avoided her and Mitzi like the plague. I'd expected to receive a call from Elaine about planning my housewarming party, but there was radio silence. I presumed she maintained distance in deference to Jace. Even Ethan was reticent when he came by to collect payment on my All Trades invoice. Justifiably, the newspaper exposé left thorny feelings in its wake. Seeing Ethan to the door, I bit my tongue at the compulsion to inquire about Jace.

I'd had my share of nosey stares during the rare occasions I left the cottage. Though I knew in time another scandal would come along and supersede mine, after Ethan's visit, I took to my bed. Jace's anguished expression when he walked into my bedroom haunted me. My duvet up to my chin, I replayed the scene over and over in my mind, conjecturing how I could've handled it better and imagining an alternate ending.

When my phone pinged late one Saturday night, my stomach jumped into my windpipe. Could it be Jace? I grabbed the phone, disappointment welling when I found it wasn't him but Fee. I'd evaded her calls and texts for weeks, but now it looked like she was done tiptoeing around me.

If you don't call me this instant, I'm driving to the airport and hopping on a plane. I'M NOT JOKING.

Tough Love Fee was a force to be reckoned with—I knew she'd make good on her threat if I didn't toe the line. I dialed her number. When she answered, I croaked, "Hi."

"You sound like crap. When was the last time you ate?"

"I've been subsisting on a diet of cashews and zero sugar cola." I lifted my can of soda and drank. "It's all I have at the cottage, but I can't go to the market. What if I run into Jace?"

"You'll have to at some point."

I didn't answer at first. Instead, I chewed a fingernail, a nervous habit I'd picked up. "I've decided to become a recluse."

"Kit." She sighed. "I get that you're depressed, but you've gotta snap out of it."

Resentment blossomed in my chest. "I'm on vacation, aren't I? I'm allowed to be a slob."

"But we agreed you'd contact Sandra Daniels and offer her a job with the new Landis-Philips branch. We agreed you'd look for office space," Fee reproved, asking, "Have you even bothered to study for your licensure?"

"No, I bought a TV, and I'm streaming 80s shows while lying in bed—I'm on season three of *The Scarecrow and Mrs. King.* In case you're interested, I think it was a criminally underrated program."

"And what about your exams?"

"I can't sit for them 'til November because of residency rules. Allow me to grieve losing the love of my life, will you?"

Fee softened. "I'm concerned about you—you're usually resilient. What about a Tele-therapy appointment with your shrink?"

"She doesn't practice anymore," I said, my throat aching with tears. "Just give me a few more days, okay?"

"Monday you will get out of bed, shower, and eat a proper meal. Deal?"

"Fine! You win." I sniffled. "Deal."

Monday came, and I did what I promised Fee. What else was there to do but heed her advice? Jace had moved on… why shouldn't I?

It was an exercise in futility. With no appetite, I'd dropped weight. My clothes hung on my frame. The simple pleasures that once brought me joy no longer appealed. I couldn't read. My tears blurred the words on the pages. The majesty of sunsets over the Atlantic? They meant nothing if I couldn't view them with Jace. The ocean had always comforted me, but now I kept the windows latched and the blinds shuttered.

Through it all, Fee was dogged about keeping tabs on me. Not wanting her on my neck, I went through the motions. I studied online guides to bone up for my licensure exam. I called Sandra Daniels, spiriting her away from Coast Realty and tasking her to scout out locations for our offices. She secured space in an office park being built down the road from Shoreside. A Landis-Philips branch would launch in the spring.

The pieces were falling into place. I should be grateful—I had more blessings than many women. Yet my heart yearned for more. I wasn't the type to feel lonely, but that's how I felt without Jace and Penny. Lonely and miserable.

Fee was an expert in assigning me jobs. She requested photos of the cottage, obliging me to tidy before taking them.

I snapped several of the patio with the outdoor table and umbrella set she'd bought me before I went inside to take interior photos. My bedroom now had a plush rug under the bed and sago palms flanking the French doors. The guestroom awaited its first guest, the quilt and decorative pillows on the iron bedstead from Gibson's.

The hall bathroom turned out exactly as I'd wanted, with the fixtures and tile work looking as if it were original to the cottage. In the kitchen, I angled to get all of the cabinets in the frame before taking closeups of the appliances and backsplash.

Jace's table was gorgeous and paired well with the upholstered chairs I'd chosen. It complemented the sideboard, too. Mellow light fell on the polished grain, and I skimmed my fingers over it. I felt connected to him when I touched it.

Shaking off my gloom, I finished my photos in the parlor. Capturing the whole room, I went around and snapped photos of the built-ins decorated with nautical-style bric-a-brac, the model of a Cutty Sark on a shelf, and the oatmeal-colored sofa with the assortment of throw pillows.

You should be proud, Fee responded upon receiving the images.

I didn't feel proud. I felt empty as a shell.

I TOSSED and turned that night, sleep elusive. I drifted off around midnight. At 3 a.m., my bladder woke me, prompting me to drag myself from bed and stumble to the bathroom. On my way back, I stubbed my toe on the dresser. "Ouch, dammit!"

I dropped to the mattress, rubbing my bruised toe. What was that noise? I stilled, listening.

Getting up, I turned on my bedroom light. Disbelieving what I was seeing, I blinked. The hallway was flooded, water flowing from the bathroom. It was inches from spreading into my bedroom. "Oh, no!"

I flicked on the hallway light and peeked into the bathroom. Water gushed from the pipe under the sink. The shutoff valve had broken off and was on the floor. My pulse thundered as I sloshed through the water to the kitchen pantry, where the main shutoff was located.

Dropping to my knees, I grasped the valve and twisted. Nothing. Marshaling strength, I tried again. *Nada*. It was too tight.

Thinking fast, I dashed for my bedroom. My cell was under my duvet. Adrenaline coursed through my bloodstream, making me shake. Should I call Jace? My guts knotted at the thought, but I hungered to see him.

Before I could reconsider, I placed the call. It went to voicemail. Opening my messages, I typed out a text and sent it. Water soaked into the rug. I groaned, hurrying back to the knob in the pantry to keep trying to turn it off. I'd give Jace two minutes to respond to my text. If he didn't, I'd call the All Trades after-hours emergency line.

My phone chimed. I seized it, reading Jace's response. *Can I help you?*

Cottage flooding… plumber you sent messed something up. I can't get water main off!

On my way. Will bring Shop Vac.

Abandoning the shutoff, I went to the bathroom, pulling towels from the linen cupboard. I put them on the floor to sop up the water, but there was too much of it. Racing to the en suite bath, I grabbed the towels there, layering them on the hallway floor. Feeling wobbly, I went to sit on my bed. I should've eaten dinner.

Once I caught my breath, I went to the bathroom and looked in the mirror above the sink. I was pale and drawn, with dark circles under my eyes. I grabbed my makeup bag, applying face powder then blush. With only moments until

Jace arrived, I pulled off my ratty T-shirt and threw on a sleeveless cotton nightie trimmed with lace.

Jace knocked on the kitchen door. When I let him in, my gaze skated over his wrinkled tee and jeans, his mussed hair. For a millisecond, my heart sang at the sight of him, then a stab of sorrow hit my chest. Without a glance at me, he strode into the pantry. Feeling fidgety and timid, I followed.

He twisted the valve then sat back on his heels, saying quietly, "It *was* too tight. My apologies. Can you show me the origin of the leak?"

I sagged against the pantry wall, running a hand over my face. My limbs were unsteady. Would I pass out? "Aftermath of an adrenaline rush," I said through rubbery lips. "And I didn't have any dinner. Now that I think about it, I can't recall if I ate lunch. My appetite has been nonexistent since our quarrel…"

Sympathy flitted across Jace's features. He got to his feet, gathering me in his arms. He carried me to the parlor and set me on the sofa. Leaving me, he disappeared, returning with a bottle of whiskey and a tumbler. He poured two fingers and brought the tumbler to my lips. "Drink."

CHAPTER THIRTY

THE WHISKEY BURNED AS IT TRAVELED MY ESOPHAGUS AND pooled in my stomach. Angling my head back on the sofa cushion, I rested my eyes. I must regain my composure—I was still much too woozy to speak coherently.

Jace took the tumbler. I heard him pour more whiskey, then there was the sound of him drinking. His voice husky, he divulged, "I've been irate since we broke up… barking at everyone, acting like an asshole. Even Ethan's walkin' on eggshells around me."

That snagged my attention. Turning my head, I probed his face. The parlor was dim, with little light spilling from the hallway fixture. Despite the darkness, his tortured expression was plainly visible.

At least I hadn't been the only one in agony. The knowledge was cold comfort.

"I should've contacted you after I simmered down, Kitty."

My heart squeezed, and I gulped away the lump clogging my throat. "What would you have said?"

"That Ma always called me a chip off the old block because I'm tenderhearted and prone to sensitivity, like Pop was. He wasn't ashamed of it, and neither am I—there's no weakness in it." Jace inhaled then exhaled, not meeting my eyes. "However, I might've overreacted. I might've judged you too harshly."

"It's not as if I set out to deceive you, Jace." I willed him to understand. Could I make him understand? I was determined to try my damnedest. "It wasn't an elaborate, calculated plot to screw with you. I wish you'd get it through your thick skull that the last thing I wanted was to hurt you or your family."

"Perhaps, but that doesn't alter the fact that I *was* hurt. When I saw the newspaper and put two and two together, I felt like a moron. Kitty was Katrina, the girl at the lighthouse. The one who got away." His lips twisted. He shook his head, guzzling another dram of whiskey. "After you disappeared, I scoured social media to track you down. Not having your last name, it was useless. I gave up. Convinced myself you were a figment of my imagination. Why didn't I recognize you at the cottage?"

I sat up, longing to touch him. I clasped my hands in my lap instead. "I've changed a lot. I've worked hard to distance myself from Katrina. To be a stronger, more confident person. Poised."

Continuing as if I hadn't spoken, Jace said, "I stopped by the *Observer*'s office and confronted the editor. I read him the riot act. Ballsy of him printing that rubbish when All Trades had an ad account with them—*had* being the operative word." He turned mournful. "I thought we shared somethin' special that night, Kitty. We'd made a date. Why'd you stand me up?"

"We did share something special." Jace's gaze bored into me. Getting unsteadily to my feet, I went to the French doors. The moon reflected on the rippled surface of the Atlantic, silvering it. I explained about returning to the cottage upon leaving him at the lighthouse. How I learned my grandfather squandered a family fortune which had taken generations to accrue. That the following day before we flew home, I'd spotted Jace with a bikini-clad blonde at the pool and balked. "Only after visiting your house did I realize my so-called rival was your sister. All I can say in my defense is I wasn't in my right mind that day at Shoreside."

The parlor was silent as Jace processed what I'd said. Finally, he asked, "What happened after you left the Cove?"

"Grandmother did everything in her power to quash stories about our fall from grace—begged, pleaded, called in favors—but Boston society made a meal of it." My voice broke. I wrung my hands. "Moving from Nob Hill into an apartment wasn't far enough away. Grandmother wanted to flee the city. As if we could afford that. We lived in abject poverty. It was beneath my grandparents to work, and who would've hired them at their age? I landed a job at a fast-food joint, but we were hand-to-mouth. That humbled Granddad. He turned to liquor, hocking what little we still owned to buy cheap rot-gut. He died from alcohol poisoning that winter. I found him on the kitchen floor after a double shift."

Jace came to stand behind me, the warmth from his body radiating like a furnace. "Jesus."

I put my forehead against the door, saying dully, "Grandmother's forgetfulness worried me for months. I suspected the onset of dementia, but she was lucid enough that losing Granddad wrecked her. She suffered a stroke, became bedridden. I cared for her the best I could."

"I don't know what to say. Your story is tragic. Traumatic." He clicked his tongue. "You were only a child."

His compassion was my undoing, triggering memories I'd buried long ago—they came in flashes. I couldn't suppress them any longer. The dread that was a constant companion in those days. The helplessness of knowing I'd be short on rent again. Subsisting on beans and rice. Hiding bills in a shoebox because I couldn't stomach the sight of them. Granddad stretched cold on the peeling linoleum. In the depths of grief at his funeral, where I held Grandmother upright while she wept. Spoon feeding her when she was confined to bed. Of her withering away, nonverbal and emaciated. I curled my fingers on the trim around the window panes as waves of pain threatened to bring me to my knees.

Jace put his hands under my elbows, supporting me. "Tell me how Katrina Randcliffe transformed into Kitty Landis."

I pulled away, clumsily pivoting on my heel to face him. Tears cascaded down my cheeks unchecked, but I didn't care. My pride was gone. "I took another job answering phones at a realty. Between that and the fast-food gig and tending to Grandmother, I was drowning. I knew it was an untenable situation. There was nobody coming to save me—no knight on a white charger—it was up to me to fix it. A college degree seemed an impossibility, but real estate classes were within my reach.

"Fee was a classmate. She was trying to better herself, too. We bonded. Got jobs at the same real estate brokerage. When Grandmother passed, I sold her wedding rings, and Fee and I disappeared to California. I reinvented myself, using my father's last name."

"Wouldn't the Randcliffe name have given you a leg up?"

"How? My grandfather lacked business acumen. People would assume I did, too. I had to sever the connection." Anger bubbled in my gut, bitterness souring it. "Not to cry poor little rich girl, but being a Randcliffe was a liability. Even when I was an heiress, my life sucked. Your family isn't like mine was, Jace. You haven't a clue!"

"But look at how far you've come. You clawed your way back on top. You're the very definition of self-made." I allowed Jace to lead me to the sofa, his arm around my waist. There was a box of tissues on the trunk from Gibson's that served as a coffee table. He dispensed a bunch, placing them in my hand. "You've restored honor to the Randcliffe name. That's admirable."

I murmured my thanks and blew my nose. Unburdening myself was therapeutic, leaving breathing easier, but I felt as limp as a wet rag.

"Is this the first time you're talking about this?"

"No. Fee knows my history. I saw a psychiatrist for a while, too. I just don't like talking about my life, dredging it all up."

"My God, you're a remarkable woman, Kitty. I can't get over how you've accomplished so much on your own."

It was time to lay it all on the line. Worrying at the tissues I held until they were ragged, I confessed, "You said before I'm guarded. That's because I don't trust easily, but the minute we met, I trusted you. I fell in love with you, Jace."

He perched on the edge of the sofa, his elbows propped on his knees and his palms cradling his head. "I've committed to the partnership with Clint, Kitty. I've signed the paperwork. I can't move to California, and I sure as hell can't ask you to relocate here full-time. You shouldn't compromise your career after all the effort you put into building it."

A shoot of optimism took root, vining its way up my chest. "Are you saying you feel the same about me? That you love me, too?"

"Of course I love you, woman. I've loved you from the beginning," he said glumly, "but I just don't see how we can make it work. How can we possibly have a future living on opposite coasts?"

"That Sunday, when I planned to tell you I was Katrina Randcliffe? I had other news as well…"

"News?" Jace straightened, hope splashing across his face. "What news?"

"I'm staying at Kingfisher Cove, permanently. Landis-Philips Agency is establishing a branch here," I murmured, emotion sticking in my throat. "I want us to have a second chance."

"Are you serious?"

"Yes, Kingfisher Cove is my home. My heart brought me back to where I belong—to this place. To you."

"But… we're worlds apart, Kitty. I'm never going to be a millionaire. I can't provide that sort of lifestyle for you."

"After everything I told you, how can you think I'd want a man who makes millions?" I demanded, shaking my head. "The trappings of wealth don't interest me. Never did."

"You deserve so much better than a woodworking plumber from Upper King." He grazed my cheek with his knuckles. "I'm a nobody. What do I have to offer you?"

"Yourself," I whispered. "All I want is you, Jace. Isn't that crystal clear by now?"

He took my hands in his. Brought them to his lips. "I spent the last weeks kicking myself for letting my male pride —my ego—blind me, but I was punishing myself as much as I was punishing you. Can you forgive me?"

His words were like music to my ears. My gaze drinking him in, I said, "You are *everything* to me… my past, my present, and my future."

He gathered me close, stroking my hair. "Do you believe in fate, Kitty?"

I gripped Jace tight, vowing to never let him go again. "I do now."

EPILOGUE

Kingfisher Cove, South Carolina
Memorial Day Weekend, The Following Year

It was the first anniversary of Jace and me reuniting. We cruised along Starfish Avenue in his crew cab, him behind the wheel and me in the passenger's seat. Penny sat behind us in the backseat, her head out the window and her tongue lolling as she watched the opposing traffic tool by.

My hair was in a tortoiseshell clip, but the wind buffeted through the cab, making strands fly in my eyes. I repositioned the clip, sighing in contentment as we approached Shoreside Resort. It was the sort of day I couldn't get enough of—warm but not muggy, the sky cerulean blue and studded with fluffy clouds, and the air soft as silk.

It was a day rife with possibilities.

Jace slowed, halting at the resort's scrolled gates where a line of cars waited to enter. A cop in the middle of the road directed the stream of vehicles flowing in and out, his white-gloved hands indicating which lane should stop and which had the right of way.

We were waved forward, and Jace accelerated. So… we weren't visiting Shoreside. Where *was* he taking me? "You're absolutely positive there's nothing I can do to persuade you to reveal where we're going?"

Jace's lips twitched with amusement as he negotiated around a slow-moving BMW then merged back into our lane. "Nope."

I reached to palm his knee. Trailing my nails up his thigh, I arched an eyebrow. "Not a single, solitary thing?"

Jace's expression was scandalized. Imitating Dustin Hoffman in *The Graduate*, he said with mock seriousness, "Ms. Landis, you're trying to seduce me."

Tilting my head back, I laughed. "Would it work? I'm dying of suspense over here."

"No, ma'am. You've already had your way with me once today," he teased, returning his gaze to the roadway. "Allow me to recover before you jump my bones again, will you?"

"*I* jumped *your* bones?"

Jace chuckled. "Woman, what else would you call slipping your hand down my pants?"

"I'd call it a… a proposition." Thinking about that morning, a delicious shiver coursed through me. We'd been fixing to leave the cottage to set up for tomorrow's cookout at Elaine's, and I'd suggested a quickie. Within minutes, Jace had me pinned against the kitchen wall with my skirt pushed up and his jeans around his ankles.

It had been hot. Sinful. Toe-curling.

Jace must be remembering our encounter, too. Bringing my hand to his cheek, he nuzzled it. The familiar rush of arousal zapped me straight to my core.

I'd expected the fluttery feelings of attraction to lessen with familiarity, but they hadn't. If anything, our familiarity made our attraction stronger. More intimate. Even sharing a simple look could make the air charged, make my body tingle.

We just couldn't seem to get enough of each other.

When we passed the new, state-of-the-art industrial park that would house the Kingfisher Cove branch of Landis-Philips, Jace said, "Not much longer 'til we arrive at our destination. How about you find something for us to listen to on the radio?"

My stomach growled as I browsed through the channels, reminding me breakfast had been ages ago. "I hope your surprise includes lunch. I'm starving."

"You'll have to wait and see."

I decided on an oldies station. "Under the Boardwalk" by the Drifters began, and we sang along with the words.

When Jace flicked on the blinker at the turnoff for Hollby Lighthouse, I glanced at him, a question in my eyes. "What are we doing here? It's closed for the holiday—we won't be able to get in."

Shifting into park at the gated entrance, Jace unbuckled his seatbelt and rooted for a key in the center console. Winking at me, he confided, "I made arrangements with the caretaker."

"Oh?"

Hopping from the truck, he unbolted the metal gate that blocked access to the lighthouse's parking lot then climbed back into the cab. "I'll pull through then lock up again."

With the access gate secured behind us, Jace drove up to the gift shop addition attached to the lighthouse proper. There were parking spots designated for the gift shop employees. He chose one, cutting the engine.

"What do you have up your sleeve?" I asked when he came around to the passenger's side of the truck and opened my door.

Jace didn't answer. Instead, he held out a hand, helping me from the cab. "I have to grab something from inside. I'll meet you and Penny at the beach."

During my absence from Kingfisher Cove, a wide set of

stairs with an attached metal handrail had been cleaved into a section of the cliffs beyond the gift shop. The stairs led to a cleared area below the cliffside. Sand had been dredged there to fashion a beach. I let Penny out of the truck, and she followed me down the stairs.

At the last step, I bent to unfasten the strap on my sandals. A plucky seagull landed on the handrail next to me, its beady eyes watchful. Penny barked at it. When the bird took flight, she gave chase.

I picked across the powdery sand to where the waves broke at the shoreline. Warm water lapped my toes. It felt heavenly. In the distance, there was the sound of a horn as one yacht alerted another of its presence. Having lost interest in the gull, Penny found a stick. She scampered over to me, and I threw it into the surf for her to retrieve.

Sensing Jace, I turned. He was spreading a blanket on the sand, a wicker picnic hamper on the ground. He'd also removed his shoes. The wind ruffled his linen shirt, exposing his taut, muscled abdomen. There was no question about it. Jace was damn sexy.

"Lunch by the sea?" I asked, joining him. "How romantic."

"I thought so." He grinned, explaining, "I brought everything by yesterday and stashed it in the staff fridge. Wine?"

"Yes, please." I sat cross-legged on the blanket and unclasped my hair clip. Jace poured a generous serving of red wine then handed me the glass. I took a sip. It was a Malbec, full-bodied and tart, tasting of plums and cherries. "This is wonderful."

"I'm glad you approve. There are chocolate truffles for dessert." Sitting beside me, Jace unpacked the hamper and prepared a plate for us to share—cheese, fruit, and crusty bread. He selected a piece of melon, offering to feed it to me. Conscious of the heat in his gaze as he watched me, I took a bite. Juice trickled down my chin. Leaning into me, Jace licked it off, his tongue tracing the outline of my mouth. Lunch forgotten, we kissed.

When we broke apart, I whispered against his lips, "Thank you for organizing this. It's perfect."

Jace fed me tidbits of cheese and bread. Between the two of us, we finished the bottle of wine, and the truffles. After our meal, replete, I closed my eyes, lifting my face to the sun. Gratification floated over me, and I sighed.

Life was truly beautiful.

Penny trotted up to us, shaking seawater from her coat. The droplets flew everywhere. Wiping our faces off, Jace and I laughingly scolded her. Her expression sheepish, the vizsla settled at our feet.

Jace stretched out on the blanket with his ankles crossed. "Come here."

I cuddled into him, using his arm for a pillow. "Are you happy?"

Jace's arm tightened around me. "Yes."

"Me, too," I said. "I feel so blessed."

"Ditto." He played with my hair, running his fingers through the strands.

I continued, "Not only do I have Randcliffe Cottage, I have you, Penny, and your family. Although I miss Fee terribly, Mitzi's been a good friend. And Sandra has become a friend as well. The new branch is opening next week. And your career is thriving. I'm pleased it's working out well for you, Jace."

"I lucked into that contract making custom cabinets at Shoreside. That job'll keep me busy for months." I felt his mood shift, then he fell silent.

Figuring he was mulling his relationship with Ethan, which still hadn't fully recovered, I said, "He's coming around. Just be patient with him."

"You're always my biggest cheerleader, encouraging me to keep the faith." He craned his neck to kiss my forehead.

I yawned, nestling into him. "All that wine. I'm drowsy."

"Take a nap."

I drifted into slumber. When I woke, Jace was spooning me. With a smile, I flipped over so we were face to face. I apologized for sleeping so long—judging by the position of the sun, it was late.

The rays washed Jace in a dusky halo, making the flecks in his irises glimmer like rare gold. He brushed a tendril of hair from my temple then skimmed my cheek with the pad of his thumb. "You know, Kitty, this last year has been the best of my life. I don't know what I ever did to deserve it."

The tenderness in his expression was nearly my undoing. My sinuses prickled. I cleared my throat, trying to fight back my tears. "I firmly believe we were always meant to be together. It was written in the stars."

"Hold that thought." Jace whistled. "Where is she? Penny! Come here, girl."

Confusion knitting my brow, I sat up. "Is something wrong?"

The obedient dog raced to her master's side. She wore a red ribbon around her neck. A ring hung from the ribbon—a diamond ring in a platinum setting.

An engagement ring.

My eyes flew to Jace. The realization of what was happening hit me, and my pulse quickened. Of course I'd thought about marrying him—I'd even considered what type of dress to buy and what sort of food to serve at the reception. However, I'd hesitated to broach the subject with him, preferring to allow it to happen organically. I'd told myself to live in the moment. To enjoy each day as it came without expectations to fulfill. "Are you popping the question?"

"Shh!" Jace chuckled. "Let me say my piece."

He praised Penny, removing the ribbon from her neck. Unknotting the ribbon, he pulled the ring off of it and placed it in his palm. The sparkling diamond was bordered by sapphires and centered on an intricate, filigreed band. It was gorgeous. "We've talked about how I make a lot of my decisions—by letting the universe guide me?"

I nodded, my heart clenching at the love I saw shining in Jace's eyes.

"All I know is forces beyond our control—beyond our comprehension—have worked their magic to bring us back together. We're soulmates. Of that I'm certain. We should never, ever be apart." Jace took a deep breath. "Will you be my wife, Kitty Landis?"

I flung my arms around him, nearly knocking him over. Peppering his face with kisses, I said, "Yes!"

"Yes?"

"The answer is yes. A trillion times yes."

LATER THAT NIGHT, after Jace had fallen asleep, I got out of bed and exited the cottage through the French doors. Penny, my constant companion, trundled behind to keep me company.

Everything was still, peaceful—there was no noise other than the roar of the ocean or an occasional cricket chirping. My bare feet sank into the sand as I strolled down to my beach. Arms crossed, I considered the stars in the sky, the same stars I'd wished upon as a teenager.

My wishes had come true.

Jace was mine, and I was his.

I murmured my gratitude to God, fate, the universe—whoever, whatever—for bestowing us a second chance at love. It wouldn't be for naught.

Pulling my phone from the pocket of my pajamas, I tapped out a text to Fee. *You around by any chance?*

Seconds later, my phone chimed. *I'm here. What's up?*

So, something happened to me today, totally out of the blue. Biting my lip, I waited. *Any guesses?*

After a beat, Fee answered, *Way to draw it out, Kitty.*

LOL

Will you spill the beans already, for pity's sake?!

With one more look at the stars, I responded, *I'm getting hitched in October, and I want you to be my maid of honor...*

THE END

AUTHOR'S NOTE: If you enjoyed *Romance at Kingfisher Cove*, please consider leaving me a review on Goodreads and Amazon. Thank you for supporting indie authors!

ALSO BY ANNE LUCY-SHANLEY

Enjoy this excerpt of *Mayfly Hollow* by Anne Lucy-Shanley

Chapter One

Wrapped in a towel and her chestnut-colored hair still dripping from her shower, Kate silenced the staccato alarm clanging from Ben's phone. The sky showing through the slats in the window blinds had transformed to something between charcoal and pewter gray, signaling she was behind schedule. She nudged him impatiently. "Get up. I gotta get to work."

"My head's killing me," Ben grumbled, nestling further into his pillow like a hibernating bear. Kate flung back the duvet, prompting him to groan and flip on his back.

Grabbing her comb from the bedside table, she ran it through her hair then gathered it into an elastic band. "Hope you're not getting that flu everyone's talking about."

Ben stretched, as if savoring the delicious feeling of the

morning after a well-deserved screwing. "Too much wine last night, more like." Hauling himself up, he sat at the edge of the mattress and rubbed his sleep-smudged eyes, his shaggy hair disheveled.

Kate selected a printed blouse from her closet. As she thumbed through the stack of laundry on a chair in the corner of her bedroom for jeans, she said, "Last night was fun. Same thing next week?"

"Sure. I'll even let you be on top."

Kate snorted, side-eying him. She scooped up Ben's tee and sweatpants from the floor and lobbed them at his head. He ducked, snagging his clothes with his fingers but not losing his grin.

Zipping her blue jeans and stepping into loafers, Kate peeked at her cell. Wincing at the time, she hastened to locate her purse and keyring on the dresser. She said over her shoulder as she left, "Lock up when you leave, stud. If you stop by the shop later, I'll buy you an éclair."

Her partner was at Buttercream Bakeshop when Kate arrived, a catchy pop song blasting over the speaker of her smartphone. Blonde-haired and blue-eyed, at forty Rosie was a decade older than Kate but exuded the perkiness of a college co-ed. She bopped to the music as she leveled flour in an eight-cup measure, adding it slowly to the whirring commercial mixer with practiced movements.

Kate projected her voice to be heard over the din. "Good morning, Rosie. Sorry I'm late. What are you working on?"

"The shortbread for Les's catering order." Rosie lifted her chin toward the ovens. "I've got the pies going for LuAnn."

"You're a lifesaver!" Kate went to the staff coffeemaker on the worktop and poured a cup of coffee. Blowing on the surface, she took a sip then grabbed the spiral bound notebook from its place beside the coffeepot, consulting her to-do list. She put a line through *Pies—three peach, three apple, three mixed berry, three cherry* for LuAnn's standing order at Corner

Market and set about assembling the pâte à choux pastry for the éclairs to go along with Les's shortbread.

Over the next hour, the two women mixed and baked doughs and batters in tandem without speaking, operating with efficiency honed over years of sharing a workspace. When the rolling metal racks were filled with trays of cooling confections, they sat for a quick coffee break, sharing the reject pieces of shortbread that had broken during cutting. Popping the last morsel in her mouth with relish, Kate savored the buttery taste. "You want to deliver orders or open the shop today?"

"I'm in the mood to deliver." With a swift look at the wall clock, Rosie pulled the elastic netting from her head and fluffed her bangs. "It's almost six! I've got to get those pies boxed and loaded into the van. When I get back, I'll run the dishwasher and bake the cookies and cupcakes."

Resigned, Kate stood. "And I need to get the case stocked before Bud pounds on the door for his breakfast. I could set a watch by that guy."

Kate yawned as she replaced her stained beige baking apron with the pristine bubble-gum pink serving apron embroidered with a cupcake logo. It was the same graphic as on the pink-and-black striped awning above the street entrance to the bakery. Pulling off her hairnet, she ran a shrewd glance over her appearance in the mirror inside the swinging kitchen doors, wiping a smudge of flour from her nose.

The trays of blueberry, banana nut, and apple cinnamon muffins were artfully arranged in the glass case beside decorative stands piled with shortbread, éclairs, and croissants. On her way to the front door to turn the *closed* sign over to *open*, Kate pushed the power button on the boxy three-burner Bunn coffeemaker on the counter behind the case. The rich, nutty aroma of brewed French Roast mingled with the hint of sugar in the air. She straightened the chairs around the half-dozen bistro tables in the shop while listening to WPAL's morning show broadcast on the wall-mounted TV.

Through the plate-glass window the tangerine orb of the sun peeked above the horizon, the sky infused with lavender and fuchsia. Kate didn't need to hear the forecast to know it would be a pleasant spring day. The international news briefing had just begun when the bell above the door tinkled. Bud Bradley, her favorite customer, entered the café.

The pouches under Bud's eyes were pronounced and his greeting less robust than normal. "Mornin', Katie girl."

"Hey, Bud. Rough night?" Kate poured his coffee and used plastic tongs to put a blueberry muffin on a paper doily-lined plate. He wearily lowered his large frame to a chair at his designated spot overlooking Main Street.

"Whoa," Bud muttered, putting his hand to his temple. Kate's forehead wrinkled in concern as he abruptly got to his feet, his actions erratic. He put a palm up to discourage her from bringing his order. "All the sudden I'm not feelin' too bright. I'm gonna have to pass on breakfast, kiddo."

"Yeah, that's probably a good idea. How 'bout I lock up shop and drive you home before you keel over?" She hurried around the counter to help Bud, untying her apron as she walked, but he waved her away before she reached him.

"No—don't get close to me. Maybe I'm comin' down with that nasty flu I heard about on the news." He jerkily pushed his chair in and went to the door. "I'm gonna crawl back into bed, where I 'spose I oughta have stayed to begin with."

Bud's face became ashen, and his fingers trembled on the doorknob as he gripped it. Kate's tone revealed her alarm when she protested, "I really think I'd better drive you—"

"Now, Katie, don't fuss! I'll be right as rain tomorrow mornin' and ready for my muffin first thing."

Mouth pursed, Kate watched as Bud staggered out to his rusted pickup and drove away. She sanitized everything he'd touched, her attention cutting to the anchorwoman on WPAL-

TV saying, "Concerning reports coming in this morning as the yet-unidentified strain of influenza cases grew exponentially the last twenty-four hours…"

Chapter Two

Still disturbed by Bud's departure, Kate worried whether she should've insisted on driving him home. Shaking off her lingering misgivings, she wrote the day's offerings on the shop's chalkboard wall above the coffeemaker. She had just stepped down from her stool when she heard the bell above the door. Turning, Kate tucked the chalk marker in her apron pocket and pasted on a welcoming smile.

Her smile slipped when she saw Dierdre Harcourt making her way across the shop.

"Kate, darling!" Dierdre was in her seventies with smooth face-lifted features. Her blue-black hair was arranged in a chignon, and she wore riding pink that made it seem as if she recently dismounted from a thoroughbred horse. "I'm desperate for your assistance!"

Irritation rose in Kate's breast, crowding out the unease that nagged at her after viewing the morning news. "Let me guess… catering order for bridge club?"

"No, Ladies Circle. Millie was to hostess, but she's under the weather, so the task falls to me, I'm afraid."

Kate's focus shifted when she noticed Ben's green Jeep Cherokee parked in front of Buttercream Bakeshop. He emerged, freshly showered and shaved, wearing his customary dark suit. When he came into the bakery, Kate briefly met his eyes. "Dierdre, do you remember when I told you last time that I'd have to upcharge last minute orders?"

"I know, and I surrender myself to your mercy…" Dierdre

appeared properly chastened, glimpsing over to Ben where he joined her at the display case. His fair brow was furrowed as he studied the chalkboard, like he was trying to decide between a muffin and a pastry. "Benjamin, how are you, dear?"

"Good day, Dierdre," Ben replied, mouth quirking, the dimple in his cheek surfacing. "I'm just fine. Thought I'd grab breakfast on my way to court. I have a hearing in a half-hour."

"Please, do go ahead of me. You absolutely must if you're in a hurry. My insignificant gathering pales in comparison to the magnitude of your vocation as a public defender."

Ben and Kate met eyes again. She could tell he was amused by the way the corners of his eyelids crinkled. He swept a hand in a gallant gesture. "Ladies first."

Dierdre flashed him a coquettish look and said to Kate, all business, "No sheet cake. The Ladies Circle gals are a discerning bunch."

"Uh…" Kate's heart sank. She knew what that meant. "Not macarons?"

"I hoped for an assortment of macarons, truffles, and petit fours. Two dozen of each."

Kate suppressed her displeasure and thought fast. "I can do chocolate truffles, and white cake for the petit fours, but I'm only able to do two flavors of macarons. What were you thinking?"

"Pink and yellow."

"So strawberry and lemon? A dozen each? And pink and white icing for the petit fours? I'm afraid it'll be quite costly at this late hour, Dierdre." Kate threw out an astronomical figure, but Dierdre didn't balk at the price. She clapped her immaculately manicured hands in delight.

"Accommodating as ever. You've swooped in and saved the day, Kate. You'll be sure to deliver to my house by ten tomorrow morning?"

"Certainly." Kate grabbed an order pad and hastily scrawled Dierdre's selections. The woman was notoriously *forgetful* about paying the invoices Kate sent via mail. "However, new bakeshop policy dictates prepayment on catering orders."

Dierdre opened her designer handbag and rooted around, producing a matching wallet. "Can I get one of your delicious croissants to take away as well?"

When the shop door closed behind Dierdre, Kate rolled her eyes. Ben roared with laughter, leaning across the counter and lacing her hand in his. "What was she wearing? There can't seriously be a fox hunt planned in Clayton's Corners."

"All she needs is a riding crop."

"Tally ho and all that rot," Ben said in an exaggerated British accent. "Our very own Lady Grantham."

"Lucky us."

He lifted a shoulder. "At least you'll make bank on her order, luv."

"I'll also be here all night," Kate groused, nonchalantly pulling her hand away. "I promised you an éclair, didn't I?"

"Yep." Ben's voice was neutral, but she sensed his disappointment as she plucked the pastry from the case with tongs. She avoided his gaze while putting it in a pink wax paper bag adorned with the shop's stylized cupcake logo.

Ben was three years ahead of her in high school, so they'd known each other only superficially then. Last year, they'd met again at a local bar called Cahoots and hit it off. Their friendship-with-benefits suited Kate to a T.

"Coffee?" Kate lifted a pink-and-black striped to-go cup, and he nodded.

When she handed him his coffee, Ben pinned her with a serious look. "When are you going to let me take you out on a proper date?"

Kate bit back a groan. She scanned his fair hair, slicked back neatly from his forehead, to his handsome, boyish face, and his broad shoulders encased in his power suit. Most women would be thrilled to date Ben. He was a catch and on a fast track to a successful private practice. He was a hell of a nice guy to boot—Kate just wasn't interested in dating. Her heart fluttered as she searched for the right thing to say. "It works. Why complicate things?"

"Because I *like* you," Ben murmured, his sapphire eyes sad. "I want more than a once-a-week-roll-in-the-sack."

"Please. Let's not get into all that..." Kate realized she fidgeted. She seized the spray bottle of cleanser and a paper towel and set about swabbing at the already spotless countertop. "You know I'm a loner."

"Yeah. I get it." Ben's fingers tightened on the wax paper bag he held, but his face remained impassive. "See you Thursday."

Conflicted, Kate observed him leave. His stiff shoulders and ramrod straight posture made his frustration clear.

Ben had a huge family. Sisters and brothers and nieces and nephews. They went to church together. Planned birthday parties and hosted ham suppers. Ben's folks had been married forty years. He'd said more than once that he wanted the same for himself someday and couldn't fathom why Kate didn't. Raised by her older sister after their parents' death, Kate didn't know how to act around Ben's family—what to say in their presence. How to belong.

Anxiety closed her throat when she contemplated explaining *why*. Could she verbalize how she felt like an actress tripping over her lines? That she was a fraud? Kate shook her head. Nope. That's why she didn't do families. It was easier to be alone. Her past was too complex to dissect.

If only Ben would accept her wishes.

"Deliveries are *finito*," Rosie said as she came through the swinging kitchen doors, tying her baking apron over her sweatshirt. "Something unusual though. Corner Market was shuttered. I tried LuAnn on her cell, but she didn't answer. I let myself in with the key she keeps hidden by the service door and left the pies on the counter with a note."

"What? Corner Market isn't open for business? That's not like LuAnn." Kate put her hands on her hips and worried at her lip with her teeth. "You don't think she's sick with that flu going around?"

Rosie volleyed her a blank look as she affixed a hairnet over her blonde curls. "What flu?"

"Instead of streaming music, you ought to listen to the news occasionally, Rosie," Kate chastised, picking up the TV remote by the cash register to choose a cable news channel. "Maybe the media is making a bigger deal of it than they should, but Bud looked awful when he came in earlier. He was so sick he had to turn around and leave."

The TV host interviewed a taciturn epidemiologist who said, "The origin of this particular strain remains unknown. The WHO is tracing patient zero somewhere in Southeast Asia. Details remain murky. There's been conjecture that it originated as few as thirty-six hours ago. Since it's already here, we know it's highly contagious and aggressive—"

The broadcast was gone, and the president appeared onscreen, seated behind his desk in the Oval Office. "My fellow Americans, it's with great gravity I address you today. Last night citizens began falling ill in massive numbers along the southeastern coast. I've spoken with state governors, and we are coordinating a nationwide shelter-in-place effective six o'clock Eastern Standard Time. I urge you to refrain from panic buying—"

Rosie's cell phone trilled from her trouser pocket. Still watching the TV, she fished for her phone. She glanced at Caller ID, then at Kate, paling. "It's the middle school."

Alternating between the president's address and Rosie's conversation, Kate's guts turned to ice. Perhaps all the hubbub was justified—she'd seen enough disaster movies to be worried. Propelled by Rosie's unsteady hands as she spoke to the school nurse, Kate moved to lock the shop door and flip the *open* sign to *closed*, adrenaline making her wobble. She had shucked her apron and was flicking the power switch on the coffeemaker when Rosie ended the call.

The distress Kate felt was mirrored in Rosie's eyes. She whispered, "I've got to fetch the twins. Robbie's got a fever of a hundred and four, and Jeff's asthma is kicking up."

Chapter Three

Kate stood in the middle of the kitchen, tapping her thigh with an index finger. She was at a loss. Rosie had flown out the back door to go pick up her twins from school, but Kate couldn't focus on any one distinct task.

Her stomach gurgled, which made her think about food. She didn't have many groceries at her townhouse. Should she go to Corner Market? Take provisions from the bakery? She'd have to transfer the baked goods from the display to the freezer first. Kate consulted the clock. It was nearly eleven. She grabbed the pad of paper from the worktop and made a list. The first thing was *freeze items in display case*. Once that was done, she called Dierdre.

Voicemail picked up on the sixth ring. Kate explained that due to the shelter-in-place mandate, she'd put a refund in the mail for Dierdre's catering order. Sealed envelope in hand, Kate was unlocking the front door when her cell rang. It was Ben. "Where are you?"

"Still at work. Why?" She stuck the envelope partway in the pink mailbox attached to the black-painted brick storefront.

It was like Kate was invisible. People strode by, frowning, their steps purposeful. A woman brushed Kate as she went by, saying crossly to her companion, "At least we have some time to shop before the lockdown nonsense. Talk about over-reacting."

Ben asked, "You know I'm friends with Jocelyn Stein, the Deputy Commissioner at the Department of Health, right?"

Kate latched the door then leaned a shoulder on it. "You've mentioned Jocelyn. What does she say about this flu? Is it really *that* bad?"

"Worse than bad. People are dropping like flies." Ben sounded rattled, which wasn't like him at all. That gave Kate pause.

"But people die of the flu every year, don't they?"

"Within hours of contracting it?" Now he was annoyed, even angry. "You have to understand—we have a vaccine for seasonal flu. We don't for this strain. Joss says they think this stays airborne for at least an hour. *An hour.* You need to wear a mask when you leave the bakery—do you have one?"

"I don't think so. I have a scarf, somewhere, that I can tie up… God, this is *surreal*."

"Wear it. And wash your hands. Or use hand sanitizer, in a pinch. You can wear gloves as long as you're careful not to cross-contaminate." There was commotion over the line and then dead air.

"Ben? You there?"

"I'm here. Driving. Fuckin' insanity on the road. Idiot almost broadsided me!"

"Be careful," Kate urged. She craned her neck to witness the activity at the end of the block. It was Mr. Gonzalez from the Mexican Grocery and a middle-aged ash blonde woman with a stiff, helmet shaped hairdo. It was hard to tell what was happening, but he was trying to take something from her. Had she stolen from his store? She kneed Mr. Gonzalez in the groin before running off. He crumpled to the sidewalk in a fetal position. Pedestrians scurried past without helping.

"Some lady just attacked Mr. Gonzalez! Let me see if he's alright. Hold on."

Phone held to her ear by her shoulder, Kate unlocked the door but stilled when Ben shouted, "Don't! I mean it. Don't interact with anyone. They could be asymptomatic. Fuck. I'm swinging by for you. We're going to my parents' farm. My family is rallying there."

Predictably, Kate's first instinct was to withdraw. She said emphatically, "No, Ben. I can take care of myself."

"I don't want to argue about this. Now's not the time to assert your independence."

"If I go anywhere, I should drive to Colliers Junction to be with my sister." Quarantining with twenty strangers was out of the question. Even dealing with her stuffed shirt brother-in-law would be preferable.

"Colliers Junction?"

"Upstate New York."

"Oh, right. Where you grew up. But that's hours from Clayton's Corners. You'd have to take I-81. Could be dicey. I'd use back roads, but what if you have a breakdown or run out of gas?"

"I filled up yesterday…" She heard raised voices outside the bakery. An Asian fellow no less than eighty quarreled with a middle-aged man whose arms were filled with packages of toilet paper. The elderly man wagged a finger at him but was prodded aside with an elbow as the younger man plowed by and continued down the sidewalk. The fellow massaged his sternum with the heel of his hand, scowling. He caught Kate's eye and shook his head in disgust.

"Kate?"

"Two men were arguing about *toilet paper* outside Buttercream," Kate murmured, chewing her thumbnail. It was inconceivable. People were acting like animals!

"Get away from the windows. You don't want to draw attention to the bakery. I've heard reports of looting on the radio." Ben paused. "Look, I'm about to turn off Route 9. I need to know whether to turn left to come get you or right for the farm."

Kate hustled through the kitchen to the matchbox-sized office she and Rosie shared, her mind racing. "You go on to your folks' place. I'll manage."

Ben exhaled noisily. "Stubborn as usual. Promise me you'll drive straight to your townhouse. That you won't leave unless absolutely necessary."

She put her hand behind her back, crossing her fingers. "Sure. I'll text you later, okay?"

Kate found the emerald-green pashmina she'd bought because it matched her eyes hanging on the back of the office door. Her whole body was shaking—her blood sugar must be low. She went to the commercial fridge in the kitchen and chugged orange juice from the carton.

Think. Think! She pulled out plastic bags with handles from the supply shelf and filled them with items from the fridge and walk-in freezer. Frozen juice and frozen fruit. Eggs. Heavy whipping cream. She scrounged through the cabinets and found nuts, seeds, dehydrated fruit, chocolate, granola.

Folding and tying the scarf over her face, she loaded the bags in her black minivan. The alley was silent, but voices echoed from a block over. Somebody screamed. Heart hitching, Kate went back inside and washed her hands with soap. The urge to move was overwhelming. She thought about the men fighting over the toilet paper and carted the unopened packet from the supply closet to the van.

Kate hefted a fifty-pound bag of flour and wrestled it into the trunk of her van, followed by a smaller sack of sugar. *Boy, I'm gonna feel dumb if I have to bring this stuff back once things settle down.* Still, erring on the side of caution, she snagged a box of vinyl gloves and the economy-size bottle of hand sanitizer when she left.

She pumped sanitizer into her palms and rubbed them

together before getting behind the wheel. Slouching in the seat for a minute to gather herself, Kate pulled the scarf down and took a deep breath. She was starving. Tearing open the bag of granola from the passenger seat, she scooped a fistful and shoveled it in her mouth, washing it down with a half-full bottle of water she'd left in the cup holder the day before.

Kate started the van and tuned to radio WVIA. Half-listening to the news, she drove to the end of the alley. The streets were nearly deserted now—barely anyone was about. She turned right onto Main Street. Bud lived on the outskirts of Clayton's Corners, east of the Save-A-Bunch discount store. Kate wanted to check on him.

The westbound highway was much busier than her eastbound side. Kate wondered why. Traffic clogged as she approached Save-A-Bunch. She braked so the car ahead of her could turn into the shopping center. Vehicles queued at the gas station on the other side of the street, extending into the roadway and obstructing the flow of traffic. People filled not only their automobile tanks but gas cans. Drivers in line were impatient as they waited, laying on their horns and yelling out their windows.

Kate's mouth parted. At Save-A-Bunch's double doors, crowds of shoppers swayed like weeds in the wind as they pushed and shoved. A truck beeped behind her. Starting, she gave the driver an apologetic wave, but with a roar of his engine, he veered around her, using the grass shoulder and kicking up dirt and rocks. He gave Kate the middle finger as he edged in front of her van.

Trembling, Kate put her foot down on the accelerator, anxious to reach Bud's house, and ultimately her own. She'd never been to his place, but she recalled him telling her about his distinctive mailbox on Sprindle Avenue. There it was! The metal cat-shaped mailbox was painted bright orange. The plaque that hung from its neck read *Bradley*.

At the end of a lengthy gravel lane was a boxy ranch with

faded tan siding. Bordered by overgrown greenery, the dwelling had a neglected air. Bud's pickup sat in front of the attached garage. Parking, Kate tied the scarf over her face and slid on a pair of vinyl gloves from the bakery.

She pounded on the front door, peeking through the glass inserts. She could see into the living room, but there was no sign of life. "Bud?"

On impulse, Kate tried the doorknob. It was unlocked. The door squeaked on its hinges as it swung inward. She hesitated before stepping over the threshold. It felt wrong to enter uninvited, like she was an intruder. The house reeked of wood rot and mothballs—and something unidentifiable. Foul. "Bud?"

He lay prone in the hallway. His skin was waxy. Coagulated trails of blood and mucus oozed from his eyes, nose, and mouth. There was a puddle of slimy liquid on the cracked linoleum floor beneath him. A repugnant stench drifted up, unlike anything Kate ever smelled before. Saliva and gastric juices pooled on her tongue. She tried to swallow them away.

Staggering out of the house, Kate yanked her scarf off. Bending at the waist, she retched into the grass. Partially digested granola projected from her mouth and nose in vile, viscous chunks. Kate's eyes watered and her sinuses and throat burned from the acid. Her abdominal muscles painfully contracted until there was nothing left to heave.

To be continued...

Mayfly Hollow is available on ebook, paperback, or read free with Kindle Unlimited.

ABOUT THE AUTHOR

Quirky hermit. Crazy cat lady. Fan of the Oxford comma.

With degrees in education and psychology, Anne Lucy-Shanley is a novelist based in the American Midwest. An enthusiast of all things romance, she also dabbles in dystopian, young adult, and non-fiction writing. As a firm believer in happily-ever-afters, contemporary romance remains her favorite genre.

Some of Anne's pastimes include drinking whiskey, sharing dirty memes, and coming up with captivating storylines while soaking in the tub. When not embracing the quiet life with a book and a cat on her lap, she occasionally travels with her husband of twenty years.

Anne loves connecting with her readers. Come join the fun at her Facebook reader group, the Saucy Society, or sign up for her monthly newsletter, The Saucy Gossip.